BLOOD
SUCKER

BT Rockwell is an author, online magazine contributor, music producer, and audio engineer from Brooklyn, New York.

At just twenty-one years old, Rockwell co-founded the DJ-based record label Tableturns. Eventually, after becoming Wu-Tang member Raekwon the Chef's personal engineer, he helped to oversee the monumental sequel album *Only Built 4 Cuban Linx... Pt. II*, which most critics ranked as the best hip hop album of 2009.

Blood Sucker is Rockwell's sophomore novel. His first, *Burn Me Up Fast*, was released in January 2015 to stellar reviews.

Exploring universally introspective concepts within urban and countercultural lifestyles, Rockwell's tales are often centered on the joys and pitfalls of current-day New York City, as well as the search for knowledge of self.

BLOOD SUCKER

www.BTRockwell.com

For inquiries, interviews, or reviews, please contact info@BTRockwell.com.

Editors: Megan Fox and Paul Weisser, Ph.D.

Book Layout: Eli Morgan and Paul Weisser, Ph.D.

Cover art: Josh Vanover

Photo credit: Chuck Robinson

ISBN: 978-0-692-95575-8

BLOOD SUCKER

BT ROCKWELL

Money was never a big motivation for me, except as a way to keep score. The real excitement is playing the game!

—Donald Trump

The bank is something more than men, I tell you. It's the monster.

—John Steinbeck,
Grapes of Wrath

One

Black was all Ira could see as he slowly walked deeper into the abyss. Deeper into the network of tunnels—the bowels of Grand Central Terminal. Pieces of trash whirled around in the air as a 6 train screeched by on the next track.

Buddha said all life is suffering, he bitched to himself. *I got ulcers. Arthritis. Nightmares.*

Eventually, Ira turned left and, exerting what strength he still had, opened a thick steel door with its rusty lock popped off.

"Keep it movin', ya shit eater! I oughtta skin ya alive," a menacing voice said from the dark.

"Calm down, Tommy Boy. It's me," Ira said after hearing the unmistakable sound of a switchblade flick open. "And let's turn on the lantern and shed a little light."

Ira struck a wooden match and lit a dented-up antique train lantern. He looked tattered and tired. Like he had been through the ringer. A Baby Boomer born in '58, but the pronounced frown lines above the bridge of his nose and natty silver hair aged him by at least ten years.

Tommy, blind and resembling a homeless Ray Charles with tortoiseshell framed shades, was sitting on a ragged foldout chair, munching from a Styrofoam container.

"Sorry there, Ira." Tommy rested the container on the dingy cement floor. "Usually I can sniff ya out a mile away. But these pork chops is all I can get a whiff of."

Ira spotted a rat scurrying toward Tommy's dinner. Its sheer mass was startling, and its dark coat and long tail were unsettling. Tommy had noticed it, too. He could hear the faint pitter-patter getting closer. Jabbing his switchblade with precision, he made the rat squeal as it darted off. The old blind man put away his blade, picked up his Styrofoam container, and proceeded to eat a dry piece of pork.

"Man, if you starve to death in this city, you surely ain't know how to survive," Tommy said as he licked barbeque sauce off his filthy fingertips. He lowered his sunglasses to the tip of his nose, showing his sightless eyes, and added, "You bring what I asked for?"

"Here." Ira handed over a bottle of castor oil.

"Once a month. It clears the system right out." Tommy smiled. "Keeps an old geezer feelin' clean. Regular. Don't worry, pal. I won't dare down it now. I ain't gonna make you deal with my tootin' and shittin' all night. I'll find a crapper tomorrow above ground." He passed Ira a fifth. "For your troubles, my friend."

The two took turns swigging in a dank bunker once slept in by the men who originally helped build the tunnels. It was claustrophobic and unforgiving, but it had walls and a ceiling. For the time being, it was home.

"Let's blast off," Ira said, crouching next to Tommy. He lit a crack rock already packed in a glass straw-shaped pipe and assisted his companion with a fix.

"Oh, yeahhh," Tommy said with relief as he exhaled. "Before this BS was around, we snorted Peruvian flake. That good shit. Goddamn Reagan. *Ray Gun*! Puttin' crack on the street so cheap. How could we say no? I ask you *that*, Ira."

"I don't know, Tommy Boy. I really don't."

Two

A gust of winter wind harshly smacked Ira across his face at dawn, as he shuffled through the nasty wet recycling bins left out on Avenue A. Oddly enough, this was a twisted form of meditation for him. The Zen of finding 5-cent bottles. Of making money.

The Zen ran off his body like cold rain, though, after observing a couple of young professionals—one accidentally bumping him as he walked by.

Their thin ties. Nooses around their weak scrawny necks, Ira thought bitterly.

He gave a nod to a shrunken elderly Chinese woman who was carrying blue plastic bags swollen with cans on the ends of a mop handle she rested on her wee shoulders.

She's tougher than these douches in their cheap suits and shirts from Men's Wearhouse, he thought to himself.

$

Ira stood on a dreary line behind many squalid homeless people who were trying to collect a few bucks from the recycling machines at Food Emporium.

After collecting his daily pay from the machine, he scrounged half a cigarette that had been stomped out on the sidewalk.

I still got my mind, he thought. *I mean, it's bruised and battered, but I can still think. And I'm as smart as they come. At least, I used to be.*

$

Gray skies brought a midday drizzle. Ira sat on a wooden bench in East River Park, drinking from a fifth of Raspberry Burnett's hidden in a brown bag. He lit the last part of the stoge he had picked up earlier and blew a series of smoke rings.

"Hey," a young man no older than twenty said, hopping off his skateboard.

Ira said nothing.

The young man kicked his board into his hand, took a seat next to Ira, and nonchalantly sparked a blunt. There was a soothing silence as they watched a thin fog consume the ever-growing skyline of industrial North Williamsburg.

"Want a lil' puff, Pops?" he asked Ira, zipping his coat and adjusting his backwards Supreme hat. "Rough day?"

Ira looked over suspiciously, but couldn't turn down the offer. He dropped the cigarette he had burned to the filter.

"Yeah, alright, sonny. I'll take a toke."

Pulling a hit as big as his lungs would let him, followed by three more, he passed back the blunt half-done.

"Damn, Pops!"

"You offered." Ira guzzled his vodka until it was nearly finished. "What's your name, kid?"

"People call me Champ."

"Oh, yeah? Why's that?"

"Because when I was sixteen, I laid out an off-duty cop who was beating on one of my boys. The cop was drunk and got suspended. Folks in my neighborhood started calling me The People's Champ. I guess it was shortened to Champ along the way. You?"

"Ira. People call me Ira."

Champ took a lengthy and deliberate look at the unkempt man. "I feel like we've met. Like this isn't the first time."

"I get around."

Champ stared even harder. "Does the name Scotti's mean anything to you?"

"I haven't heard that name in years. I loved Scotti's."

"Yup," Champ said, taking a puff from the blunt.

"On Broadway, right? Mmmm, they had the best minestrone. And the fried calamari? To die for." Ira gazed off as if lost in a memory of a glorious Italian feast.

"Yup," said Champ. "You got it."

"What *about* Scotti's, huh?"

"Silvio Scotti is my father."

"Unbelievable," Ira said. "Fuckin' unbelievable."

"I remember you. From the restaurant. My dad would always boast how accomplished you were and shit, after you walked out. Like you were the man. But you—"

"I know, kid." Ira looked at the pavement below. "I know. How *is* dad?

"Sick. Leukemia. He doesn't have long."

"Sorry."

"Where'd you go, anyway?" Champ asked. "I mean, I thought you and my dad were sort of tight. At least at the restaurant. Then, one day, we never saw you again. *He* never saw you again."

"I guess I got sick too, kid. Ya know what I mean?"

"Makes sense."

"What are you doin' with yourself these days?" Ira said, changing the subject. "You in school?"

"I'm a junior at CUNY Hunter."

"Oh, yeah? I did a SUNY back in the day. What's your major gonna be, huh?"

"Economics."

"Huh! You don't look like one of those nerds."

"You, neither," Champ said, clipping the blunt.

Thoroughly stoned, they watched the East River Ferry serenely cruise by, heading south, as the light precipitation petered out.

"Well, listen," Champ said, "it was good to reconnect. I'm glad you're still ticking. Maybe I'll see ya around."

"Maybe," Ira said. "Maybe."

"Take care of yourself. I'll give your regards to my father."

"You do that, kid."

Champ jumped on his board and skated away into the mist as fast as he had come.

Three

At the East River Esplanade, a mere ten feet away from the cars and commercial trucks whizzing by on FDR Drive, Ira stood facing a corroded garbage can with a fire roasting in it. Huddled next to him under the moonlit sky were Henry, Missy, and Oscar—three others utterly down on their luck, desperately trying to find warmth. Sharing a bottle of booze, they hoped to heat their insides in a way the fire in front of them couldn't.

"Jesus Christ, Henry! Don't chug it all, ya troll!" Missy yelled in a raspy voice. A cheap cone hat was strapped to her head and festively tilted to the side.

Henry, hunched over from MS, and looking disgusted, said, "Happy New Year to you, too, Missy. Bitch! You don't own me."

"I own that gin!" Missy shouted, out of breath. "So slow your roll, troll! Ya pig!"

"I'll show *you* pig," Henry said. He sloppily swigged from the bottle, causing the cheap liquor to spill from his mouth. "Oink! Oink!" He passed the bottle to Ira, who took a sip and handed it to Missy.

"This winter's colder than a witch's titty," Oscar said, rubbing his chapped hands together. "My digits are so bone dry, I can't stand it."

"You're gonna have to," Henry said. "December wasn't any fun, but wait till February comes to get us."

"You need a nice pair of gloves on those paws of yours," Ira said.

"Yeah, stupid," Missy rudely said in her horribly gravelly tone. "Get yourself a pair like these." She showed off her worn mittens.

"I want a pipin' hot shower," Henry said. "Or a warm soak in the tub."

"A bubble bath," Missy half-mumbled.

"Hey!" Oscar said. "That reminds me."

"What?" Ira asked.

"I got something to show you guys. A New Year's Eve surprise that won't disappoint." Oscar pulled out a dime bag patterned with Nike swooshes and dangled it in front of the others. "Just do it, heh, heh, heh."

"What the hell is it?" Missy asked.

"Bath salts," Oscar said. "My nephew slings this shit and gave me a taste for the holidays. It's what's hot in the streets. My nephew ain't never steered me wrong yet."

"Oh, yeah?" Henry asked.

"Yeah!" Oscar answered definitively. "Let's snort it—see what happens. Maybe we'll smoke the rest."

"I'm in," Ira said without hesitation. "What a way to welcome in the new year."

"I want some, too," Missy grunted.

Henry nodded.

"Here," Oscar said. "Let's see your wrists."

Ira took off his glove, and Oscar carefully poured out the bath salts.

The next time Ira could form somewhat cohesive thoughts, he was standing in the middle of First Ave, a couple of miles from the roasting green garbage can fire. The bath salts had taken their effect and had him running away from himself. But no matter where he ran, there he was. Then came the vision.

"I'm a Viking!" he proclaimed at the top of his lungs. "A fuckin' Norseman! No! A Norwegian god! Ha! I'll rule this crummy world! Ha ha!"

Drunken bystanders out celebrating in droves after the ball had dropped quickly gathered around. Snickering and pointing, they snapped pictures and shot videos with their phones that would no doubt end up on Instagram or YouTube.

"This shall be mine, you brainless saps!" Ira ranted. "You wanted to keep me down in the dirt? I'll command this glorious ship!" He leaped onto the back of a parked Ford pickup, pounding both feet with all his might as he sweated profusely in the freezing cold. "I am Thor! Bjorn the Bear! Rahhhhh!"

A heavily tattooed man sporting thick mutton chops and wearing an Anthrax T-shirt, black leather vest, and matching combat boots hurried out of the dive bar on the corner, slamming the door as he stormed out.

"Hey, sausage gobbler!" His nose scrunched up, accentuating what looked like an animal bone, pierced through his septum, as the devil's face tattooed on his bicep scowled in an identical fashion. "Get the hell off the truck! I'm gonna rip out your spleen, assclown!"

Camera phones kept flashing from both sides of the avenue.

"The light is getting brighter now! Follow the light!" Ira yelled, still stomping away on the flatbed. "You ignorant halfwits! You follow the light before you get sucked into the darkness! The dark goddamn tunnel! Goddamn snakes sent from the goddess Hel!"

The man tugged at Ira's ankle. "I'll show you darkness when I stick your head where the sun don't shine!"

"Snakes!" Ira pleaded. "Get off me, ill demons! I'll destroy you with my hammer fist! I'll kill you with my bear claws. I won't let you take me down with you to rot in the muck and mire! Not again! I want another chance!"

The convincing hallucinations of snakes and demons yanking at his feet scared the shit out of Ira as he was mercilessly dragged off the truck by its irate owner. Foaming from the mouth, Ira panicked and did what came natural at the time.

"Aaaaahhh! You animal!"

A police car with sirens blaring swung a U-turn in front of the altercation. One officer hopped out of the car immediately with pepper spray in hand. She was appalled after she pushed through the rambunctious crowd and witnessed a madman gnawing away at another man's chest right through his bloody leather vest. Her partner stepped out, gripping a baton, and swung at Ira until the Norse god lay unconscious.

Four

Ira opened his eyes. It didn't take but a minute for him to realize he was in a holding cell with a handful of degenerates. Some kept to themselves, stressing, while a pair who had clearly been busted together joked around with each other, not having a care in the world. It was impossible to tell what time it was—if it was day or night.

"Mace! Ira!" an officer called out, glaring at the prisoner. His belly sagged over his belt, pushing his pants down low on his hips. The weight of his holster didn't help. "That's you, shit head. It's your lucky day, ya sicko. You're free for now. Happy fuckin' New Year."

$

"Where's my watch?" Ira asked as he was about to be released.

"Here," the officer said, handing Ira the gold Rolex in a Ziploc. "Where'd you score something like that, huh? Sucking cock in the men's room over at Grand Central?" He looked to his partner. "Hey, Pauly. Did you hear what I asked him? I said, 'Where'd you score something like that, huh? Sucking cock in the men's room over at Grand Central?'"

His partner, unimpressed, continued reading the funny papers.

"I earned it. In another life," Ira told the cop as he put on the watch.

"Another life?"

"The old-fashioned way."

"How's that?"

"Spit polishing your mother's poontang."

"Take a walk, buddy!" the cop snarled. "Before you get a baton up your ass… for the *second* time in twelve hours."

Thirty minutes later, Ira was sitting in a booth at a diner not far from the precinct. A slightly chubby yet irrefutably attractive woman in her early forties sat across from him. She was wearing a Chanel suit, and her fiery red hair was pinned back tightly into a ponytail. The two stared into each other's eyes.

"So," said Ira.

"So," repeated the woman.

"So, who the hell are *you*?" he asked bluntly.

"And why the hell did I bail you out?" she retorted.

"Let's start with that."

A waitress came by to fill their coffee cups and headed to the next table.

"My name is Catherine Finer," the woman said, sternly. "I work for Mitchell and Jones Savings. Have you heard of it?"

Ira sipped his burnt coffee. "You couldn't bring me for a *real* meal?" he asked. "Of *course*, I've heard of M and J. I used to have an account with you when I was a child."

"Is that because of your Uncle Jeffrey?" she asked.

"Yeah. He was a founding chairman. He was also a heartless prick. Smoking stinky chewed-up cigars and shaking my hand so firmly I would whimper. He got off on things like that. Ya know—making babies cry. I also know his business practices weren't, for lack of a better word, sound."

"Be that as it may, Mister Mace, your uncle won't be shaking your hand anymore. He has passed, you see. In his sleep. Peacefully."

"Too bad."

"That he passed? Or that he passed peacefully?"

Ms. Finer asked with a grin.

"Whichever you want," Ira answered impatiently. He waved his finger at the waitress, getting her attention. "Lemme get two eggs, sunny side up. I want 'em extra runny. Add some hash browns, toast, orange juice, and bring me some more of this shit you're calling coffee."

"You developed quite the appetite from last night," Ms. Finer said.

"Look, I haven't seen this guy, my dear Uncle Jeffrey, in, well, most of my goddamn life," Ira said getting back to the point. "My father had a falling out with him when I was eight or nine, and we lost touch. So what the hell is this about?"

"Your uncle acquired a fortune over the course of his lifetime. Unlike your father, he never wed or had a family of his own. On his deathbed, he spoke with his longtime friend, Warren Buffet. Subsequently, to everyone's shock and dismay, your feeble uncle decided to leave everything he owned and had worked so hard for to be auctioned off for charity. Rolls-Royces. Monets. A stunning mansion in the South of France. Everything. Can you even fathom, Mister Mace? There was also the three billion dollars in his personal portfolio. All wasted on the faceless masses. Charities in Africa? Saving babies from mosquitoes? Rubbish. It makes me shudder."

"You wanna tell me what this has to do with *me*?" Ira asked.

"The lone thing your uncle did *not* give away were his shares in the company he helped to start. In fact, he offered a couple of his colleagues, Mister Winslow and Mister Britteridge, the sum of his shares to split between themselves. On one condition."

"And what was that?"

"The condition was straightforward enough," Ms. Finer stated. "Winslow and Britteridge could get the shares if they could hunt down his single nephew and closest living relative on the planet."

"Me?" Ira scoffed. "Nah, there must be a mistake."

"You didn't let me finish, Mister Mace."

"Please, continue," Ira said sarcastically.

"Second chances."

"What about second chances?"

"Although you were estranged from your Uncle Jeffrey, he monitored your successes and your struggles from afar."

"Is this someone's idea of a terrible joke?"

"Am I laughing? Does it look as though I'm being facetious?"

Ira didn't answer. He just sipped burnt coffee.

"He told these men if they could find you, from whatever rock you were hiding under, and give you another chance at what you *supposedly* do best, the shares were theirs."

"I can see you're excited about this plan," Ira said with a smirk.

"Or, Mister Mace, you can do what I positively recommend you do. You can decline the position with M and J, and simply walk away forever. For that, M and J is willing to give you five million dollars. Wired to your account by the end of one business day, and you can be on your merry way. If you still *have* a bank account."

The waitress returned with Ira's breakfast. He lowered his mouth inches above the plate as he shoveled in his meal.

"Nevertheless, Mister Mace, we have a lot of paperwork to deal with," Ms. Finer said, looking repulsed. "For starters, you need a crafty lawyer to make this, shall we say, embarrassing incident from last night disappear. Make everyone forget how you bit a man like an absolute savage. Agreed?"

"Agreed."

"And take a shower, will you? You smell rank."

Five

A wise man once said, "Honesty may be the best policy. But it's important to remember that apparently, by elimination, dishonesty is the second-best policy." Ira's Uncle Jeffrey wasn't an honest man. He was the next best thing—dishonestly rich. Not rich. Wealthy.

One dark day, he must've realized he had nobody, Ira thought, placing his razor on the sink. Looking in the mirror at his own freshly shaven face, he could hardly recognize himself. His hair was drastically shorter, untangled, and combed. *So he had a pity party, with me as his guest of honor.*

Wrapped in a warm plush robe and slippers, Ira walked out of the bathroom. The Georgian-style furniture in his presidential suite at the Waldorf Astoria was meant to suggest the White House. Under the gentle glow of a chandelier, a bank statement sat on a desk formerly owned by General MacArthur. Ira peeked at it to diminish any disbelief still lingering in his mind.

One million, two hundred eighty thousand, four hundred and six dollars… and twenty-three cents, he read silently to himself.

Anxiety immediately led Ira to gobble forty milligrams of diazepam and chase it down with a mouthful of vodka that had been chilling on ice.

"You ready for me, baby?" an exotic black woman called from the bedroom in a thick Haitian accent. Her head was shaved, and she was wearing nothing but red lace panties and fishnet stockings as she lay across the California King. "I'm gonna fuck your brains out."

"It's been a while." Ira put the jug of vodka back in the ice bucket and sat next to her on the soft comforter. "I'm not even sure I can get it up. I might need Viagra or somthin'."

"Baby, you don't have to worry 'bout nothin'. Maneeya is gonna make the pain go away and all the pleasure come rushing in. Right… to… here," she said, as she firmly gripped Ira's crotch. "*Kouche tande*."

Six

A few months went by. The burly NYC frost gave way to life-giving springtime.

Champ skated as fast as he could down the bustling streets of Chinatown. Holding his breath for as long as he could, he carefully avoided contact with the pungent dried octopi, live frogs swimming in buckets of water, strange prickly produce, and any other unfamiliar objects the outdated storefronts on Mott had on display. An alien land within the borough. Not only because of the chattering of unintelligible languages and dialects, but because it looked as if it had been wholly skipped over by time.

Alongside him were his best friends since grade school, Reese and Tyler. They took turns doing manuals—dodging cars and pedestrians alike. Reese ollied a fire hydrant with ease. Tyler led them into an alley, where he did a kickflip, barely clearing a mangy cat that had managed to tuck itself behind trash bags piled against the wall.

"Ohhhhhh!" shouted Champ, skidding to a stop in the alleyway.

"Holy shit, Ty!" Reese said in disbelief. "Fucking sick!"

"You were about to bite it bad," Champ said.

"And that cat was *this* close to being flattened," Reese added with his thumb and pointer finger an inch apart.

"Roadkill," said Champ.

"That close, huh?" Tyler raised his eyebrows.

"Here," Champ said, giving his boy a vapor pen packed with wax and ready to be smoked.

"Thanks, I *need* this." Tyler took a puff from the pen. And another. "Oh, my god! So tasty. Lemon Haze?"

"Yeah. I copped more yesterday," Champ replied as he grabbed the pen and took some puffs to the head.

"I think those shrooms are finally kicking in," Reese said.

"Oh, definitely," Champ said, giggling. "They kicked in."

"Let me hit that G Pen again," Tyler said.

As they started the second round of the cipher, Reese gently rubbed his glassy eyes and then stared in awe at the blackened brick wall in front of them. He lost himself in the gridded pattern the mortar had created.

"I don't think Reese needs any more smoke," Champ said, unable to control his smile from showing all of his thirty-two teeth.

"Let's skate," Tyler said after a laugh. "You guys ready?"

"Let's do this bitch!" Reese shouted awkwardly.

In less than twenty minutes, they were gliding down the smooth promenade adjacent to the East River, fearlessly avoiding cyclists, families with strollers, and clusters of men fishing with humble rods and pails.

All three of the boys were tripping hard, seeing the most vibrant of visuals and noticing little things they would no doubt usually take for granted. For instance, the rippling foamy waves pushing ahead atop the river. With a shit-grin still on his face, Champ impressively did a tailslide off one of the park benches.

$

Later that evening, the boys skated to a bodega in the East Village. A fat drunk, bald on top but with plenty of hair wrapped around his ears, was snoring away on a milk crate. A Muni Meter kept him upright, and on the pavement beside him rested a crinkled coffee cup with a few coins in it.

"You got a ten-spot?" Reese asked.

Champ handed over a crumpled bill.

Reese walked into the bodega under the buzzing of fluorescents, grabbed some forties, and placed them next to the register.

With one eye fixated on the Palestinian movie playing on his iPad behind the counter, the cashier slid his other eye in Reese's direction.

"ID," he said flatly, with complete indifference.

The picture on Reese's driver's license had him with longer blond hair than he currently had. He also looked quite young, but his birth date undoubtedly proved that he had recently turned twenty-one.

The cashier squinted skeptically before bagging each of the forties.

Brashly, the fat drunk from outside barged into the bodega in an uproar, and marched straight to the counter.

"What the hell, Arab flutternutter-son-of-a-goat?" he barked as he banged the counter with his fist. His missing teeth made it hard to understand him. "Where the motherfuck are the Colt 45s at today? Where they at, I said?"

"I already told you this morning *and* this afternoon," said the cashier. "We're out. There's plenty of beer back there. Choose another, you pain."

"Colt 45! Colt 45! Now!" yelled the drunk furiously. "Colt 45, or we got a problem, Mohammed!"

"Stinky bastard," the Palestinian said, losing his cool. "That's not my name."

The fat drunk practically shoved Reese out of the way as he leaned across the counter. "Mo-hom-med! Mohammed! Ya camel-humper! Mohammed!"

Having had enough for one day, the cashier pulled out a broomstick, which was snapped in half and sharpened at the end.

"I'll kill you, you piece of trash!" he shouted, waving the stick in the air and getting ready to lunge. "I'm warning you! Get out! You'll know when I have more for you, loser! Go get a job!"

With that, he swung the stick, purposely missing the drunk by a matter of inches, but knocking the gum rack on the countertop to the floor for effect.

"Fuck you, you Arab sand nigger!"

"It is you who is the nigger!" screamed the Palestinian. "Get out! Get the hell out of here, or I'm gonna come around there and *make* you get out! I'll plunge this stick up your shitter!"

"Fuck you!" the fat drunk yelled.

"No," said the cashier, "fuck *you*! Right up your dirty asshole!"

The disgruntled regular walked out.

Putting down his homemade beating stick, the cashier finished bagging the forty-ounces as though nothing had happened. "Thank you. Come again," he said.

To Reese's surprise, when he exited the bodega, the drunk was tranquil, snoozing on the milk crate once again.

"Yo, hold on," he told Tyler and Champ as they began walking away with their forties and their boards. "I gotta do something real quick. Get ready to book outta here."

Reese silently tiptoed up and karate-kicked the milk crate, making the drunk grimace as he landed squarely on his tailbone. By the time he knew what had hit him, the boys were skating away, laughing their asses off until their sides hurt.

"Try not drinking for a night, fucker!" Reese yelled.

Soon, they made it to a giant rooftop party. Kegs were flowing and nitrous tanks were blasting. With a red cup in one hand and a red balloon in the other, college kids were dancing to the booming beat—letting off some steam.

Champ, Reese, and Tyler sat down on lawn chairs in a corner of the roof, overlooking the LES. Tyler ate a stem from a sack of mushrooms and passed them to Reese.

Champ looked at the midnight sky. There was a new moon, but it was an extremely clear crisp night, revealing constellations normally washed out by the city's light pollution. To Champ, the stars seemed to prance around, floating toward each other and sometimes even toward him. He took a huge toke of wax from his G Pen, savoring the moment.

"Why do cubensis taste like such shit?" Reese asked with a sour face.

"Because they *grow* on shit," Tyler answered. "Duh." He vaped a hit of Lemon Haze from the pen. "Isn't it bananas—about Washington and Colorado?"

"What?" Reese asked.

"Don't you pay attention to the news?" Champ asked. "They legalized weed."

"They did?" Reese was shocked.

"Hell, yeah," Champ confirmed. "Where have *you* been? Anyway, it's a matter of time till it's legal here. Too much revenue to be made by the government. Watch. They're gonna cave eventually."

"I'll believe it when I see it," Reese said.

"I wish we could go downstairs to a smoke shop and cop an ounce of herb," Tyler said. "May I smell your finest flowers, please?" he asked politely, imagining what he would say if the day ever came. "Your sweetest cheeba, *por favor*. I'll take it all. I just wanna get high."

"Yo, is anyone else trippin' their nuts off?" Reese asked.

The three hooted and hollered under the starlight.

Seven

Ira walked through the cavernous lobby of a building located off Wall Street. Dressed to the nines, he had confidence in his eyes. A couple of men in tailor-made suits were at his side.

"Mister Mace, we're ecstatic to have you join the team," said the first suit. "We're a successful team either way, but your reputation speaks for itself. A wild card." He tittered stiffly. "Speaking of cards—here, you'll need this laminate."

Ira waved his new credentials at security before entering the elevator.

"Ms. Finer spoke highly of you," said the second suit, as they reached the twenty-third floor.

The first suit smiled, adding, "And don't worry about any blemishes from your past, Mister Mace. Americans have a short memory."

"Investors even shorter," said the second suit.

The elevator opened with a bing.

A large sign above the receptionist's desk read:

MITCHELL & JONES SAVINGS

The men walked by the front desk to the end of a bustling hallway.

"This is it," the first suit said. "I hope it's to your liking."

Ira walked into his new office. It was impeccable. Natural light shot in from the east, providing balance to the dark mahogany furniture. He hung his tweed coat on a hook and slowly sat at his grand desk.

"Can't wait to see what you can do," the second suit said. "You're kind of a legend."

"Alright, alright," said the first suit. "Let's not kiss too much brown eye. It'll go right to his head." He looked at Ira. "Listen, transitioning can be tough, but—"

"Where were you last?" the other suit interrupted.

"I've been sick for a while," Ira said. "I had to take a step back."

"Oh, yes. Sick."

"Well," the first suit said, "as I was saying, transitions can be overwhelming. Let me know if I can help you settle in. At least until you get the full swing of how we do it here."

Ira reclined on his buttery soft leather chair, not even bothering to respond. Like a sponge, he soaked in the epic view of lower Manhattan from his corner office in the sky.

"If I'm not mistaken, do you not have a meeting?" the second suit asked.

"Yes, she had mentioned first thing this morning."

$

A long table separated Ira and Catherine Finer in a vacant conference room. The suits were gone.

"You dirty dog," she said in her pinstriped skirt suit, legs crossed. "You dirty dog. You couldn't resist. *Could* you? The temptation."

Ira said nothing.

"With all the money you were offered, you still wanted our help to get back in the race," she continued. "Why not just move to Honolulu, put on a pair of Crocs, and call it a day?"

"The same reason you're across this table," Ira said calmly. "I guess I must enjoy the game. And I miss it."

Ms. Finer leaned in. "More like *addicted* to it," she whispered. "Must've been fun spending that fresh green."

"I found some things to do."

"I knew you would," she said. "This is an extraordinary turn of events for you."

"Indeed."

"That wire to your account must've knocked your socks off."

"You could say that," Ira agreed.

"We figured a small advance on your salary to get you back on your pathetic feet was in order. Chump change."

"I know what it was." Ira was starting to lose patience.

When Champ abruptly knocked on the meeting room door, which was slightly ajar, Ira's face lit up.

"Champ! Glad you came. How you been, man?"

"Good," Champ said. "Classes started and—"

"Can you wait outside, sweetheart?" Ms. Finer said. "This is an imperative meeting we're having."

Champ grinned as he winked at Ms. Finer. "Of course, hon."

"We'll keep it brief," Ira said.

Annoyed by the interruption, she shut the door in Champ's face. However, he could still partially hear the rest of the conversation.

"Let's get serious, shall we?" Ms. Finer said. "Remember, this second chance we're offering you is quite unorthodox, considering."

"I'm the best there is," Ira said.

"When you're not loaded?"

"I'm the best."

"I'm keenly aware of your abilities, Ira. VP in less than eight years. One of the modern-day architects. Giving outrageous loans that could never be paid off, while buying cheap mortgage-backed securities on the secondary market. Ripping off the American people for a living. But the bubble burst, and you narrowly escaped being indicted. *Very* narrowly." She leaned in and whispered again, "By a cunt hair."

"I told you, I'm—"

"The best," she coldly interrupted. "Yes. And what the hell were you doing out there—like a street person for these last five years? Word was you went cuckoo. Spent your savings on marching powder and lawyer fees. And then you plain lost it."

"I needed a break from the madness. That's neither here nor there, because I'm back now. I'm back."

"You *are* intriguing. Unlike the others." She thought to herself for second, ogling Ira. "We've already gone over this. This is a second chance for you. You may be the Prodigal Son when it comes to finance, but because of your, let's say, instability, we had to pull a lot of strings and call in plenty of favors from the other board members for this to work. This can go two ways. Make our lives easier or—"

"One-forty!" Ira shouted, slamming his hand on the table. He managed to regain his composure. "That's my goddamn IQ. One-forty. I don't need you to explain my job description."

"I was sent here to remind you—"

"Remind me of *what*?"

"Do your fucking job, and do it well," Ms. Finer replied. "Prove your worth. Make us sizable returns. Prove you're not a useless senior citizen. We here at M and J won't accept any less. Remember the contract you signed?"

"I remember."

"You're guaranteed one year. *One*. You can get canned the same as everyone else if your productivity doesn't meet our strict standards." She shook her head. "You couldn't just take all that free money and retire like the dinosaur you are."

"And let *you* have all the fun?"

She slid a stapled packet of papers in front of him.

The title page read:

MITCHELL & JONES SAVINGS

NUISANCE REPORT

"Read it and take notes," she said. "Not pretty stuff."

"Nope," Ira said as he perused the packet.

"Bet it gets you off good, though."

Ms. Finer slipped Ira a handwritten note before she left, giving the stink-eye to Champ, who was sitting right outside the boardroom.

Ira quickly read the note to himself. *You'll receive a message when the stars align in the heavens. The text will specify a time and place. Black tie. Be punctual. Be showered.*

Champ walked in and took a seat.

Ira flipped the note and the nuisance report. "How much did you catch?"

"Enough," Champ said. "What are you trying to accomplish?"

"Not entirely certain. I'm good at this. Nothin' else. What's a guy to do?"

Champ didn't answer the rhetorical question.

"Bet you were surprised when I tracked you down to give you my number?"

"Sorta. But I'm curious by nature." A wall of books stacked on shelves from floor to ceiling caught Champ's eye. "That's a lot of damn reading material. There must be infinite rules in your line of work."

"Too many rules for my liking. But there's always a loophole, kid. *Always*."

"So why did you invite me here, anyway?"

"I wanted to see if you'd entertain the idea of an internship with, well, me. It's an internship, but don't worry. To make it worth your while, I'll pay you seven-fifty a week. You can get class credit and put some cash in your pocket. You don't have to answer this—."

"Why me?"

"Why *not* you? You're an economics major, aren't ya? You like shekels, don't ya?"

"Shekels?"

"And because your father was always kind to me. So were you in the park."

"What would I do?"

"Whatever I ask, I guess."

"Like an assistant?"

"Not *like* an assistant. An *assistant*. Seven-fifty a week."

"I think you can afford more than that."

"Fine. A thousand. A thousand a week. Because you were generous with me. Think about it."

"More," Champ said with his best poker face.

Ira sighed in disbelief. "Jesus. Two. Two grand a week. Not a penny more. Take it or leave it."

"I'll take it."

They happily shook on the deal.

"Don't fuck up, kid."

"Same to you," Champ said with confidence.

"You might not be fully qualified or have the proper training for this position, but you're like me. You're sharp as a tack. And I can trust you."

"Why?"

"Because you're *not* like me. Get it?"

"I think so."

"Plus, I don't trust sniveling ass lickers. You're a real person. You're my man. In the future, I can make you rich." He checked his Rolex. "Okay. So take a hike. I gotta get to work here."

"Sweet Rolie," Champ said.

"You have good taste. It's worth twenty K."

"That's a whole lot of K's just to know what time it is."

"You *better* know what time it is, kid. Besides, it's classic. Built to last. And unlike most people you'll meet on this godforsaken planet, it won't ever let you down."

"Makes sense to me."

Ira thought for a moment. "What do you know about fringe benefits, Champ?"

"Extra benefits supplementing an employee's—"

"Dear lord! What textbook is *that* from? We're going out tonight."

"I got classes."

"So *after* your classes, ya pain in the ass! Call a couple of your boys if you want, and have 'em meet us, too. Tell 'em we're gonna be out all night."

Eight

Champ was seated in a lecture room at Hunter among his peers. The whiteboard in front read:

ECONOMICS – PUBLIC POLICY AND ETHICS

The young African professor at the head of the class dressed the part of his elder colleagues—corduroy pants with a sweater vest, bow tie, and sports coat. Champ was the opposite—T-shirt, ripped jeans, and Nike SBs.

"Black Tuesday," Professor Laurence stated in a stern French accent. "The uttermost notorious of days in our stock market's unsavory history. A harsh and swift kick in the rear, following the glorious Roaring Twenties. By 1927, the market had truly taken off with unprecedented growth. Why?" He pointed to a Korean girl with cat-eye glasses. "Jennifer?"

"There was growing wealth throughout all the states. More people wanted to invest their savings."

"Yes," the professor said, ever so slightly excited. "Yes, I see. Prosperity, you say. What's another reason? Proceed, Jennifer."

"Speculation?" she said, unsure of herself.

"Ah, yes," the professor said. "Speculation. Let's discuss that fascinating phenomenon. The birth of what we might call day trading. Long-term investments were becoming passé. Now we were going to get rich in a day for less than a day's work. Average people with insufficient knowledge of the market, gambling on high-risk stocks based usually on someone else's suggestion. Isn't that something? A twisted and distorted version of the American Dream. Buying on margin. Who can expand on this topic? Let's go, people. This was all included in your reading assignment."

Champ sheepishly raised his hand.

"*Monsieur Championne.* You have the floor."

"I think it was a strategy to handle investors who couldn't afford to buy stock in full," Champ said.

"And that means?" asked Professor Laurence.

"They could put, like, ten percent down and borrow the rest from other investors."

"*La bonne réponse.* Unfortunately for our poor citizens of that time, President Hoover was not a staunch believer in market regulation. Thus, buying on margin—and that includes our *own* banks, people—buying on margin was rampant, and investments in general were at a feverish high." He paused. "Then what?"

No one had a hand in the air. Only blank faces.

"Jesse…, no? Sarah? Nobody? Okay, fine. I pick you, Mateo. Enlighten us with your wisdom."

"Essentially," Mateo said with a slight Spanish accent, "as investors started to realize the stock boom was, like, in actuality an overinflated speculative bubble, they began more and more to sell and cash in, rather than buy, causing panic to set in, causing even *more* investors to sell. Quickly, the price of stocks plummeted."

"Keep going," pushed the professor. "*If* you can. Tell me about the margins, please."

"Margin debts were called in, and of course many couldn't ever be paid back," Mateo said.

"Ah ha," the professor said. "That made the value of the stocks worth even less. Margin investors who thought they were sitting pretty were instantly in massive debt. Families went broke overnight. And the banks? Tell me about the banks, Mateo."

"Many banks had been taking depositors' money and investing it in the speculative market themselves. So, due to the panic, when many people desperately tried to make withdrawals from their accounts, the banks couldn't make good and became insolvent. Hundreds of banks closed nationwide, leaving many, like, shit outta luck."

There was a scattering of muted laughs. The kind you get whenever someone curses in a classroom.

Professor Laurence looked pleased. "Impressive, my boy. I see *someone* took notes. Took this assignment with all seriousness. Okay, let's bring it home, *mes jeunes élèves*. Let's sum up this mess. That colossal and embarrassing stain on our nation's quote-unquote distinguished tapestry. What are your views regarding the crash that fiercely came to a head in the fall of 1929? This quandary our financial forefathers found themselves in? Huh? Go ahead, Althea. Take it away."

"To me," Althea said, "greed for profits without proper oversight by an impartial and preferably righteous group was the major cause for the crash."

Somehow Champ had never noticed his classmate, even though she sat only one row up and four seats to his left. Her soft facial features, strawberry-blond hair, and gentle voice practically had his tongue dangling out of his mouth.

"A simple answer, Althea," the professor said, "but poignant. Honest. And?"

"And, well, it seems to have plenty of similarities to this generation's crash from 2007," Althea added.

"Good!" Professor Laurence exclaimed. "Now, for the remainder of the class, we shall dig deeper and meticulously examine this tragic event."

Nine

That evening, Tyler and Reese were standing on the corner of 29th and Third, entertaining themselves with their iPhones, when a black Escalade with tinted windows pulled up.

Champ cracked open a window from the back seat and said, "Get in."

Tyler and Reese did just that.

"Hey now, fellas," Jerry the driver said, "we all ready to rock?"

"Let's go, Jerry!" Ira shouted. "We got a date, and we sure as fuck can't be late!"

The Escalade darted through the Midtown Tunnel, and it wasn't long before Ira and his younger entourage were at Islip, climbing the stairs into a private plane.

A stewardess with blond highlights and the body of a goddess was standing at the top of the stairs to greet them.

"Welcome, gentlemen," she said, showing off her perfect pearly whites. "Please relax and let me know if there's *anything* I can get for you. And let's have a wonderful flight."

"Where we goin'?" Champ asked.

"You'll find out," Ira answered.

Champ, Tyler, and Reese cheered like giddy schoolchildren as the jet took off.

$

A Yukon Denali was waiting for them when they arrived.

"Welcome to Miami, boys," Ira said. "Get in the truck."

Tyler rolled down the window and stuck his head out as they cruised the strip.

"South Beach! We here!" he yelled.

Palm trees. Tanned scantily clad women. Art Deco architecture on Ocean Drive, shining in an array of neon colors.

"I can't believe it," Reese said. "There *is* a god!"

"There's *me*. And you're welcome," Ira said. He lovingly put his arm around Champ's shoulder. "You girls ready to get sloshed?"

"I'm ready to get trashed with ya, old man," Reese said.

"Watch who you call an old man," warned Ira. "I'll drink your bony ass under the table."

"Where we goin'?" Champ asked.

"You'll find out," Ira said, holding up a bottle of JD. "Let's wet our whistle a little with *this* first. Who's got some ganja, huh?"

The motley crew took shots of whiskey and shared a blunt of Haze as trap music pumped from the radio. Sweet smelling clouds of smoke bellowed out of the SUV.

"Oh, shit!" Tyler said as the blunt reached the filter. "Tell me it's true! Tell me it's fucking true!"

"It's true," said Ira.

"What's true?" Reese asked.

"We're going to Wave?"

"Wave?" Champ asked.

"It's, like, the hottest spot in Miami Beach right now, man," Tyler said. "Bomb! After tonight, I can die in peace. I love you, Ira."

"Get outta the truck, boys," said Ira.

Next to them, as they piled out of the Yukon, were mustard yellow taxis idling beside a team of banana yellow Lamborghinis.

"What now?" Tyler asked.

"Ira? Is that you?" someone called from behind.

"In the flesh."

A man wearing a white linen shirt and pants approached them through a boisterous, smoky crowd. His hair was tied in a bun on the top of his head, similar to a samurai's. He had on white Prada sunglasses encrusted with fake diamonds, which must have made it hard to see in the dark of night. Fully ignoring Champ and his two pals, he grabbed both of Ira's arms and embraced him.

"Ira! It *is* you! How you been, man? It's been fucking forever!"

"Forever," Ira said. "Guys, this is Lester. We used to call him Lester the Molester, 'cause as a kid he was too touchy-feely. Always giving hugs and shit."

"And I used to call *you* Uncle Irie," Lester said. "Ha! Love it!"

"Uncle Irie?" Reese asked, amused.

"Here on the beach, everybody calls me Lee Stacks. Lester the Molester got put on the back burner. Anyhow, I'm glad Dad put us in touch after all these years."

"Lester's, I mean *Lee's* father worked with me in the good ol' days," Ira said. "Downtown. We made tens of millions together. Shit! More than that. He's a shark, that father of yours. Oh, by the way, meet Champ, Tyler, and Reese. They're my guys. I wanna show them a good time tonight. Maybe get their dicks moist. Somethin' they won't forget for a while."

"Look," said Lee Stacks, "the good news is, I can assure you'll get in the club. And I can assure you, I'll bring over some fine talent. The rest? That's on you. Let's head in."

"It looks like you're doin' okay in Miami," Ira said as they headed toward the entrance. "The party-promoting treating you well?"

Lee Stacks grinned. "My life's a fairytale."

"You look good," Ira told him. "You really do. You're a very pretty man, I must say. Love the bun."

"Shut the fuck up, Uncle Irie."

As hundreds of people stood in line, attempting to get into Wave, a bouncer in a tight black T-shirt that showed off his pecks unhooked a velvet rope and stepped aside so Lee Stacks's guests could enter.

"Get your game faces on, boys," Ira said.

The house lighting was shiny and polished. A domed ceiling was lit blue, the walls purple, and pillars separating the VIP skyboxes, gold. Naked women painted in glow-in-the-dark bodysuits were twisting and contorting on pedestals spread throughout the dance floor as if performing in Cirque du Soleil. On the far side of the club, green lasers shot out in all directions as the DJ spun tracks below. The speakers were deafening. The dance floor was turnt up.

"Make yourself at home, I'll be back shortly," Lee

Stacks told Ira at the top of a lighted staircase. "Glad you came."

Alcohol was conveniently waiting for them in their VIP skybox. A bucket of champagne. A bottle of Grey Goose. Cranberry juice.

When Lee Stacks returned, he had three young women with him young enough to be Ira's granddaughters.

"Ira," he said, "take care of these girls. They're my babies. I have to deal with a few things. Good luck."

Fake eyelashes, fake hair extensions, fake asses maybe—but the way they turned Champ and his friends hard was real as rain. One was Chinese with a sultry stare. Reminiscent of a Bond girl. She was wearing a sleeveless shirt with cream-colored bootie shorts and matching six-inch stilettos. Her two friends were sisters, whose miniskirts practically revealed their Latina *chochas*.

"Ladies, come and sit," Ira said. "Have a drink with us cool guys."

He did a bump of coke from a bullet and provided a hit for Champ, who inhaled through his left nostril and passed the bullet on down the line.

Everyone poured themselves a drink and toasted to a fantastic night.

"Hi," one of the sisters said to Champ as she pushed up on him. "My name's Roja. This is my sis, Alma.

You're from New York City, huh? I've never been. I wanna go *real* bad."

"Your dreams can come true tonight, gorgeous," Tyler said on the other side of her. He leaned in her ear and added, "We got a pretty nice ride headed back after last call."

"Last call's too early," Alma said. "You don't have to go *that* soon, do you, *papi chulo*?"

"I might never leave," Reese chimed in.

"Oooh, Pitbull!" Roja yelled. "This is the jam, yo! I wanna dance! This is my joint, yo! This is my joint!"

Ira snorted another bump from the bullet as all the others headed to the dance floor. He grabbed the Chinese girl by the arm.

"Why don't you sit this one out with me, love," he suggested. "I don't bite, sweetheart…, but I love to lick."

The Bond girl sat down, intrigued.

"What's your story?" Ira asked her.

"Mi been inna Miami fah ah year. Fi mi name ah Ruby."

"That accent?" Ira said astonished. "Where the fuck did you come from, honey?"

"Mi am Chinese, but fi mi fambily ah fifth generation Jamaican," Ruby said with a sensual smile. "Believe, dere a nuf like mi."

"Shit," Ira said, shaking his head. "You learn something new every day."

While Champ, his buddies, and the pair of sexy sisters blissfully let loose as they were showered with confetti, Ira and his Bond girl were escorted by security to a private room.

$

The Yukon was ready for them as they finally exited the club, hours past closing. Lee Stacks had made them stay to take shots of rare tequila with him and some of the bartenders.

"Hop in, boys," Ira said, shit-faced, sitting shotgun. "Let's blow this popsicle stand."

The red sun peeked its head out for breakfast as the posse found a Cuban food truck in a questionable neighborhood on the way to Opa-Locka Airport.

By the time the plane departed for New York City, the man-pack had already crashed out. The stewardess wiped drool from Reese's mouth as he snored away, then lowered the window shades to block the bright morning sky.

"And I might drink a little more than I should tonight," Tyler mumbled in his sleep. "And I might take you home with me, if I could tonight."

It was a Pitbull track stuck in his brain from the club.

Roja was splayed across his lap. Her dreams of visiting the Rotten Apple were coming to fruition.

Ten

"Is this where you bring all your first dates?" Althea asked, sitting across from Champ at the IHOP on East 14th. "Hmm?"

"Nope." Champ smothered his stack of silver dollars with strawberry syrup. "I just love pancakes."

"So, I don't know…, tell me something," Althea said.

"You first," Champ insisted.

"Okay. Ask away."

"Favorite color," he said, taking his first bite. "What is it?"

"That's your question?"

"I gotta see if you pass the color test."

"What's that?"

"Just something my Pop's taught me, that's all."

"The color test, huh?" She thought for a second before answering. "Turquoise."

"Turquoise?" Champ put down his fork and sat back in his seat.

"Turquoise…. Well, did I pass, or what?"

"With flying colors. Get it?"

"God!" She rolled her eyes. "So, what the hell *is* the color test, anyway?"

"It's actually about primary and secondary colors."

"I'm not understanding."

"See, my dad once told me that I should always ask a girl what her favorite color is before getting serious with her. If she simply names yellow, red, blue, green, purple, or orange, she's probably boring as fuck and lacking creativity."

"Is that so?"

"Or as he put it—a real snoozer."

"I guess I'm not a *snoozer*, then, huh?" she said while laughing. "Okay, my turn…. This is a big one."

"Shoot."

"What do you see yourself doing after you graduate?"

"After graduation? I see myself rolling a giant cone of high grade and getting hella faded."

"You know what I mean," she said, smiling and shaking her head.

"Right to the nitty-gritty, huh?" Champ pondered the question. "I'm not sure. I'm an economics major because I like money. And I wanna make a lot of it. Mostly because we didn't have enough growing up. What about you?"

"I think I wanna start my own business," she said.

"Like what?"

"Dunno. Something progressive. Something green. But that's as far as I've gotten."

Champ sipped his apple juice.

"I bet that sounds vague" she said. "And pretty stupid, right?"

"Not at all. It sounds virtuous."

"Thanks. That's sweet."

"It's the truth."

"But…, it's, like, tough figuring out what I wanna spend the rest of my life doing. Ya know?"

"It's a daunting thought."

"Do *you* have a job?"

"Sort of," Champ said, drenching what was left of his pancakes with more syrup.

"Sort of?"

"I'm a personal assistant."

"For whom?"

"His name's Ira Mace."

"What does he do?"

"He's a seasoned successful banker."

"How did *you* get *that* job?" she asked, dunking her scrambled eggs in ketchup.

"Why? What's wrong with *me*?" Champ asked jokingly. "Right time, right place, I guess."

"What kind of banking?"

"High finance. Truthfully, I don't know yet. I'm newly hired, and I didn't even apply in the first place. I think it's largescale accounts. Heavy stuff."

"Heavy stuff, huh? Be careful around those slick talkers," Althea said. She dabbed the corners of her mouth with a napkin. "Don't sell your soul to the almighty dollar. It's wrong. *And* it's tacky."

"Tacky, huh?" Champ was amused. "What do *you* know about it?"

"I know a thing or two." She winked. "I know a little somethin' you may never know."

"So, if not money, what's it all about?"

"Happiness. Love. Family."

Champ wolfed down the last bite on his plate, shaking his head.

"I'd put good money on the fact that somewhere there's a filthy rich family—one that's happy and loves the shit out of each other."

"I suppose," Althea said. She sipped her tea. "Look, I'm not against the rich or being rich. But I hate the idea of profits over people. Don't you agree?"

"I'm not sure what to think," he said slyly. "I'm still in school. Still learning."

"What else are you into? Besides making money?"

"Skating," Champ said, before gulping down his apple juice. "Mushrooms. Skating on mushrooms."

"How's that?"

"It's fuckin' incredible. Freedom in its purest form."

"Sounds very Zen. What else?"

"Rap with real lyrics," Champ answered. "Not like most of the garbage out there. Sci-fi novels—Jules Verne and Arthur C. Clarke. Any kick flick produced by the Shaw Brothers. Your turn. What do *you* do for fun?"

"Roller skate."

Champ burst out laughing.

"Hey, what's so funny?"

"I wasn't expecting that. That's all."

"You like using a board. I'm a lady. I like boots."

"We should have a skate date. Me? You? Skate date?"

Althea gazed into Champ's eyes. "Promise me you won't sell your soul. Pinky swear."

Champ wiped his face and locked pinkies with the engaging young woman across the table.

Eleven

Ira was throwing a party in his swanky Tribeca loft, but it was too stuffy for him. Sweaters and pleated dress pants. Evening gowns and pearls. Fine Cabernets and Caspian caviar. All the things that didn't really impress the man who threw the soirée. In fact, he was merely hosting so everyone at M and J could see who clearly not to fuck with.

Waiting in his dining room were two men in their mid-seventies, wearing three-piece suits and polished leather shoes. They seemed to be from an era long gone. One pulled out a gold pocket watch to check the time.

Somehow appearing dapper, Ira sat basing cocaine in his bedroom. On his nightstand were a plethora of prescription bottles—Celebrex, Xanax, Vicodin, and an ulcer medication. Next to the pills was a glass of red wine.

"What are we doing back here?" Champ asked, sitting on the bed. He was wearing gray slacks and a cashmere sweater over a blue button-down. He had also applied product to his hair and run a comb through it. "They're in the dining room as we speak."

Ira exhaled as he placed the pipe on the nightstand. "So what? I'm done for the night. Enough mingling."

"You *have* to see them," Champ said, waving the smoke from his face.

"Do I?"

"They obviously wanna talk to *you*, not me."

"No," Ira said. "I don't feel like going out there and dealing with those repugnant blood suckers. *You* can. I'm not in the mood."

"Not in the mood?"

"Not in the fuckin' mood, kid!" Ira picked up the pipe again anxiously. "Why do you keep questioning the big cheese, huh? Do this for me. Consider it a test of competency. Got it? You're my assistant, right? Well, *assist!*" He hit the pipe. "Tell 'em who you work for, and pray to the good lord himself they remember your adorable *punim*."

"Is that what's gonna transpire right now?" Champ asked, annoyed.

"Yeah, *transpire*, kid. Trust me. Do what I say. Let's go. March! Hut! Hut! Hut! Oh, and clear everyone out by two A.M. Understand?"

"Yes."

"And close the door behind you."

Champ shook his head before walking out through the gathering, past the string quartet playing in the corner, to the old men who were starting to lose patience in the dining room.

"Who are *you*?" one of them rudely asked Champ.

"Mister Winslow. Mister Britteridge—"

"*You* are?" Winslow interrupted.

"My name's Champ, sir."

"*Champ*?" Winslow asked. "What kind of a name is *Champ*?"

"I'm Ira's assistant. He's feeling a tad under the weather."

"Under the weather?" Britteridge asked.

"Sorry, sirs. Nonetheless, I will relay this conversation accurately to him."

"You are awfully young," Britteridge said. "Which school did you attend?"

"A good enough school to know only a dolt needs to answer that question," Champ said with his chest out. "I have nothing to prove to you."

"I love it!" Winslow's frown turned upside down. "Can he pick 'em, or what? Ira's good."

"*Damaged* goods," said Britteridge, not convinced.

"What did you gentlemen wish to discuss this evening?"

The three sat at a white marble table. An amethyst-colored crystal pendant imported from Italy illuminated the room from above.

"I trust he read the Nuisance Report Ms. Finer gave him?" Britteridge asked.

"That firecracker," Winslow added.

"She *is* a firecracker, isn't she?" Britteridge said with a smug smile.

"He read it," Champ said. "I did as well."

"Good," said Winslow. "Regarding this damn Mexican cartel, its leader has been displeased we haven't assisted him yet with our services. And he's being persistent in his request for said services. Very pushy."

"Is Mister Mace on top of this issue?" Britteridge asked.

"Yes," Champ replied. "We've already begun working on it. We don't plan on getting bullied. At the same time, M and J would love another client, wouldn't it? One with deep pockets?"

Britteridge nodded. "Exactly. This issue is exceedingly paramount to particular board members. The deal must be civil. We're not a bank of thugs, here at M and J, are we, young man?"

"It needs to be dealt with forthwith," Winslow added, seemingly working from the same brain as his old colleague.

"Understood," said Champ.

"Tell Ira we want this handled *immediately*," Britteridge said. "And with extreme discretion, you see?"

"Discretion," Champ repeated.

"We'll get you below the border for a meeting as soon as possible and wait for your analysis," said Winslow.

The two men gingerly rose to their feet and put on their long coats and old-timey bowler hats.

"Bankers," Winslow blurted out with a crooked grin. "We're quite the breed. You know what they say, Champ: Give a man a gun, and he can rob a bank. Give a man a bank, and he can rob the world."

"Tell Mister Mace, thanks for the wine," said Britteridge. "He has adequate taste."

$

Champ checked his watch once the last guests had left. It was 2:15. He knocked on Ira's bedroom door with force.

"Ira, open. It's me."

Waking from a daze, Ira wearily walked to the door and unlocked it. His tie was loosened, and his button-down was sloppily untucked.

"They all gone?" he asked as Champ came in.

"Yeah."

"Good. You get any names? Huh? Did ya?" Ira pinched Champ's cheek. "You get those names and numbers, ya handsome devil you?"

"A few."

"It's all about contacts, understand?"

"Yes." Champ yawned. "I'm beat. I'm gonna head home. We'll talk more tomorrow when you sober up."

"Says *who*?" Ira asked in a huff. "We're not done yet." He thought for a moment. "I'm gonna make a quick phone call. Let's get into some trouble."

$

A half-hour later, on his sprawling thousand-square-foot deck lit by scented candles, Ira was marinating in a bubbling Jacuzzi. His arm was snuggly wrapped around a tall, thin call girl in a skimpy baby blue bikini. He took a pinky dip of E from a small mound on a plate. The molly sent a shiver down his spine, causing him to make a face as though he had sucked on a lemon. Then he dropped a pinch of powder onto his palm, and watched the hottie in the bikini lick it clear off.

"Oh, my!" he said. "Like a cat. Meow!"

"What the heck *that* for?" she asked in a clumsy Eastern European accent he couldn't precisely identify.

"*This*?" Ira asked, nodding toward a TV remote floating in the water, sealed in a sandwich bag.

He pushed a button through the plastic bag, and a 55-inch flat screen emerged from out of the deck, triggering the girl to clap and use her two fingers to whistle.

"Champ!" Ira yelled sharply. "Hey, Champ! Come out here and get in the water! A hundred-four degrees! Perfect! Let's go!" He looked to the prostitute, who was sipping from a glass of Cabernet. "Your adorable friend must've done a number on my boy."

"Is he your boy for real?" she asked.

"Yeah, whatovit?" Ira said, slurring his words.

Champ slid open the screen door and walked out onto the deck, followed by a young lady with heavy eyeliner. This one was much shorter than her co-worker—maybe five-feet tall without her heels. Her curves and giant fake boobs were hard to ignore.

"Hey, hey," Ira said. "There they are. Have fun? With…with…?"

"Kelly," the girl said.

"Kelly!" Ira shouted. "Was Kelly's pussy worth the price of admission?"

Champ blushed.

"Oh, you must've sucked all the words right out of his penis, huh?" Ira said.

The girls both giggled as Champ's face turned a darker shade of red.

"Now get in the water," Ira insisted. "I'm tellin' ya—it's a hundred-four degrees."

"Okay, already," Champ said, wearing shorts he had borrowed from his boss.

Ira swiftly climbed out of the Jacuzzi and threw on a towel.

"You won't need *her* where you're going," he told Champ. "Shall we, babycakes?"

Kelly let go of Champ's hand and let Ira lead her back into the loft. Champ couldn't believe it. He was appalled. But when the scrumptious seductress still sitting in the steamy water undid her bikini top and gently bit her lip, all his problems drifted away.

Twelve

"*Alto*!" one of the men demanded in Spanish.

He frisked Ira, and after that, Champ, making sure to take away their phones.

They stood tentatively on a desolate beach somewhere in Sayulita, Mexico, while a couple of dark peasant-looking men clutching machine guns leered at them. But Ira could tell these were no peasants. They were killers. Their hats protected them from the hot sun, and their bare feet were half-buried in the sand.

Ira and Champ were overdressed in Italian suits. They had assumed a conference room perhaps. Instead, they were whisked away from their hotel to the proverbial middle of nowhere.

When the pat-downs were finished, one of the men pointed toward the door of a wooden shack.

Inside, Ira and Champ took off their suit coats and sat down at a metal foldout table. The only light came from the midafternoon rays of the sun, which were piercing through the cracks and seams of the shack. A gentle knock led one of the gunmen to open the door.

In came a short, stocky Jewish man. Thanks to his board shorts and Hawaiian shirt, he looked like a regular. But even a regular couldn't avoid perspiring from his pits in the wood oven they were baking in. The man took off his brimmed hat and threw an old leather briefcase on the table, but not before waving for the men with machine guns to leave.

"How are ya?" the man asked Ira and Champ. "You have a good flight?"

"Yes," Ira answered.

"Hope the goon squad didn't spook ya too bad. They're mainly for show. My superior likes to put fear in hearts. Did it work?"

"We're fine, Mister Lipschitz," Ira said, lying through his teeth.

"You know how it is. And please, call me Leonard. You must be the legendary Mister Mace? The savant. And who's this?" Lipschitz pointed at Champ. "The young protégé? *Shalom* to you both."

"You're too kind. Since we're on a first-name basis, call me Ira. And yes, this is my astute assistant, Champ."

"Okay, Ira. Sorry for the frisk, also," Lipschitz said. "We don't mean to inconvenience. But we have to be assured nobody's listening in on our private powwow."

"Understandable," said Ira.

"And I'm certainly not gonna be recorded saying what I'm about to say," said Lipschitz. "Ya know what I mean?"

Ira nodded.

"Very well. As you're aware by now, I'm one of Señor Salazar's attorneys. Most, like myself, call him Mister Manny. Mister Manny has liquid assets he's been stockpiling at an alarmingly fast pace. Much of it in U.S. dollars. This is a problem."

"Sounds like a problem," Champ said jokingly.

"It's a *big* fuckin' problem!" the lawyer snapped. "A *big* one."

"So what *is* the problem you're having?" Ira asked.

"Mister Manny's issues center around his inability to spend. To spend freely in the international market, so he can acquire the tools and resources he needs…, needs to run a flourishing business. See the problem?"

"Yes," Ira said. "Yes, I think I do."

"Thoughts?" Lipschitz asked.

"Currently, the AML laws are relaxed," Ira said. "Even more so here in the land of enchantment. Let's face it—the cartels run the show. Corruption's rampant."

"So, how will it work?"

"In short, there are two ways we'll accomplish our goal. The first works like this: The U.S. dollars, or dirty money, Mister Manny makes in Yankee Land—get it back here across the border. Using fake identification cards, your men will make cash deposits into shell company accounts with Banco Maya, a subsidiary bank that M and J recently purchased in Mexico City. That bank can then wire large sums to additional shell companies holding accounts with M and J branches within the U.S.—shell companies owned in one way or another by Mister Manny."

"And the second way?"

"The second is in many ways similar to the first, but involves somewhat new technology in the field of electric checking and a procedure called remote deposit capture. And that's the method we'll be using much more frequently. If I did my research right, Mister Manny owns a few *casas de cambio* here, no? Exchange houses?"

"Yes," Lipschitz said. "He's a silent partner in a group of exchange houses."

"Good," Ira continued. "Mister Manny's men will use cash made from drug sales in our country to acquire money orders and travelers checks. Tons of them. Once they're smuggled back into Mexico, the exchange houses will scan the bulk checks and then send them electronically to their accounts with M and J in the U.S. Then, once again, that money can be wired to one of many legit or shell companies quietly owned by your boss. Those companies will share and recycle the digital currency until the trail back to the root becomes more and more unclear—thus, completely scrubbing the money clean as can be."

"Sounds too blatant," Lipschitz said. "I don't get it."

"That's the beauty of correspondent banking. Because the exchange houses and Banco Maya will accept those deposits, no questions asked, the corresponding banks up north rarely if ever check on the validity of the transfer. Or scrutinize the account's owner. Especially if *I* have a say in things. Look, we, as the bank, take our cut and move the money down the line to its next home. A middle man who minds his own business."

"And that's all?" Lipschitz asked.

"That's all," said Ira. "Clean American moolah in our banks, available for Mister Manny's corporations to send wherever he so chooses." Ira straightened the knot in his tie. "Drug-processing supplies, bullets, guns…, hell, rocket launchers—he can buy whatever he pleases."

Champ reached into his suit coat pocket and handed a neatly folded packet of paper to Lipschitz, who now had beads of sweat dripping from his flappy jowls.

"We also have great relationships with offshore banks around the globe, in places like Panama, Luxemburg, and the Cayman Islands," Ira said. "Offshore accounts are an excellent option. They may protect your client more thoroughly than leaving the cash wholly in accounts with branches in the States. But I'm sure you and *el jefe* are already hip to that information."

"Interesting, Ira," the lawyer said, skimming through the printouts, which contained a variety of charts and graphs. Unimpressed, he opened his briefcase and put away the stapled packet. "I can see you've thought this out," he said. "I have to admit, I was hoping for something a bit more…, shall we say, covert."

"The reality, Lipschitz—"

"Please, call me Leonard."

"Sorry, Leonard," Ira continued. "The reality is, we've run this plan in the past. It works. Mister Manny's late to the party. Who do you think helped keep the banks afloat when our market tanked? The only people willing to give the banks copious amounts of liquid spending? People not unlike your superior. *Comprende*?"

"What about *you*, kid?" Lipschitz asked. "You've been terribly quiet over there. What say you?"

Champ looked to his boss for permission and was given a subtle gesture allowing him to speak. "I think Ira hit the nail on the head. Even with prior money-laundering issues, our institution has you listed as a low-risk country, meaning your business will not be monitored as closely as somewhere like North Korea or Iran, for instance."

"On top of that," Ira added, "the Justice Department can't possibly keep track of all the transfers and business dealings made by correspondent banks every day. So, in essence, they expect *us* to help them by policing our own affairs! That's like asking a burglar to turn himself in after making a huge score! It's a joke!"

Lipschitz sat back in his chair to think as he patted his forehead dry with a handkerchief.

"We can take it all," Ira added. "I can't stress that enough. We can take it all."

"All, huh?" the lawyer said. "Overly zealous, wouldn't you say? Aren't you concerned with where the loot comes from? The majority of countries frown on such behavior, no?"

"Drug trafficking. Human trafficking. Gun running. It's gonna happen, regardless," Ira said. "Who are *we* to stop it? We take money. It's what we do. We don't claim to be noble or even principled. We take money."

Champ was made uncomfortable by the bluntness of this statement. He looked at Ira with concern, but was also careful not to question him in any way.

Ira's bravado led him to continue. "Listen," he said. "Even if our government *does* take notice for some reason, Congress has turned a blind eye to plenty of deeds M and J has done over the years. Why? Because together, the banks with the size and reach that we have, represent a prominent pillar of American society. A pillar needed in order to keep the roof from crashing in. We're simply too fuckin' big to dismantle. Too fuckin' big. I'm not worried whatsoever."

"I see," said Lipschitz.

"This will be tremendously lucrative for both parties involved," Ira said.

"Okay, fellas, let's proceed."

"Great," said Ira. "Oh, and one more thing. Try to take it easy on our employees in Mexico City. A bribe goes a lot further than a threat. Catch more flies with honey, no?"

"I'll make sure to pass on that message."

"Please do," Ira said.

"Our people will get in touch with you, and we'll begin."

"How much do you think you'll be pumping?" Ira asked.

"A billion? Who knows? Maybe two if you're as proficient as you say you are." Lipschitz closed his briefcase and stood up. "Gentlemen. A pleasure. Tweedle Dee and Tweedle Dum with the AK-47s will bring you to your driver. If we're lucky, we'll never need to meet like this again. If you're unlucky…, and please, *please* remember this…, Mister Manny *will* hunt you down." He stomped his foot on the worn floorboards. "There's more than a few schmucks buried around these parts."

Ira nodded fearlessly.

"Enjoy the rest of your stay in sunny Meh-hee-ko. And don't forget your sunscreen." The lawyer tipped his hat. "*Shalom*."

Thirteen

Ira was trapped in a dream.

In reality, he was half-naked, sprawled out on the heated tiles of his bathroom floor. The toilet bowl still had bloody puke on the rim.

In the dream, though, amidst leafy foliage, he was trapped, yet could see all from a vantage point above.

A young elk ran for its life through the forest before cutting across a field.

Is that me? Ira thought, uneasily.

The calf made high-pitched cries for help while scurrying at top speed. But it was to no avail. Four wolves were closing in from behind. In a flash, another pair of wolves revealed themselves from the tall grass in front. An ambush. They blocked off the elk so there was absolutely nowhere to run.

Is that me? Ira thought to himself in his dream. *The wolves? Am I one of them?*

The elk was yanked to the ground and chomped on the neck, causing it to bleed out. Glaring and grunting, the other wolves ripped and tore at the flesh of their fresh catch. When one of them tried to flex its dominance over the alpha, a fight broke out. Their bloody mouths snarled as they exposed their razor-sharp teeth. It was terrifying to watch.

Those wolves…, Ira thought. *Vicious…. Violent…. I'm not the elk, either…. Helpless…. Victimized…. I'm neither the predator nor the prey…. Who am I?*

Ira noticed a butterfly with orange wings outlined in black that was perched on a yellow lily. The Madrilenial, distinguished and exquisite, was sipping nectar secreted from the base of the lily's petals. Indifferent to the concepts of anguish and agony, it did not feel sorry for the elk. Nor did it condemn the wolves for ruthlessly slaughtering another one of god's creatures solely for their own gain.

Satisfied with the sweet nectar, but ever hungry for more, the butterfly took flight, hovering over the fresh kill. While the wolves tussled and fought for meat, the Madrilenial gracefully landed on the elk carcass and sucked its blood. Why? Because it could.

There was a beep in the distance, followed by another. Ira awoke to a text message on his phone, which was lying next to him on the floor.

The message read:

> 417 Park Avenue - Apt. 13F
> Thurs., May 15th @ 9 PM
> AURUM

Fourteen

"What are we doing here?" Champ asked Ira.

Still in their work attire, both were facing a modest two-family home in Red Hook, as Jerry the driver sat parked across the street in the recently cleaned and buffed Escalade.

"Huh?" Champ said.

Again Ira didn't answer. Instead, he opened a screen door, walked past the kitchen and into a cramped room, where he flicked on the light. It was a baby's room—filled with a crib, dolls, and a changing table.

"Funny this room has a crib in it," Ira said.

"Whose place is this?" Champ asked.

"Not important," Ira answered. "The difference is, my crib was oak. Very stable but no frills." He pointed to a corner. "And I think it was *there*."

"Was this *your* room?"

Ira ran his finger along the predominately pink and princess-themed mural on the wall. "Believe it or not, my mother birthed me right in this room."

"Bullshit."

"There was a snowstorm. A blizzard. They didn't have a snowball's chance in hell of making it to the hospital by the time the contractions got real."

"That's bonkers."

"In any case, this was my room. All mine. I was an only child. Yup, all mine..., until I was sixteen."

"Wow." Champ soaked in how tiny the bedroom was—at most, ninety square feet.

"Yeah, wow. I know there are people in a desert somewhere burning cow dung to keep warm..., and yeah, they may have it worse, but... sixteen *years*. So much fuckin' time in this room.

"Where the hell's the family who lives here now?" Champ asked.

"I paid 'em to clear out. I wanted to chat with you for a bit."

"Are you serious?"

Ira didn't bother answering the question. "I saw how you stared at me in that shack in Sayulita. That look of concern. Almost disgust. You're not the first who's given it to me. Judging."

"I wasn't judging, Ira. I—"

"This is how we make bookoo bucks, kiddo. You have the potential to get in on the ground floor. A chance most of these geeks born with silver spoons in their mouths could only dream of. I can help you get rich with the snap of a finger. I'm talking a millionaire before your twenty-fifth birthday. Ten mil by your thirtieth! The good life. There's a catch, though, Champ. There's sacrifice involved. You could lose your soul. Or, more likely, it's still there, but has gone faint due to neglect."

"Is it worth it?"

"That's for you to decide, kid. I made my bed. I gotta lie in it. Luckily, the kind of illegal I do is pretty damn easy to avoid criminal charges."

"Did you ever do anything besides make money?"

"Like skateboarding?" Ira gave Champ a condescending wink.

"You were in the Peace Corps. Seventy-four through seventy-six. In Peru and Venezuela. You lied about your age so you could volunteer abroad."

Ira was caught off guard. "Oh, yeah? Where'd you get that?"

"Wasn't difficult," Champ said. "Your Wiki page."

"Listen, you're talking about another lifetime ago. Ya understand? I was a dreamer. We all were. That was the mood in those days. That was then. This is the now. And, now's a time to make a whole lot of cheddar. Live like a prince. Buy your own island."

"Manhattan's an island," Champ said.

They both smiled in agreement.

"I brought you here to explain a few things. See, I swore to myself once I could leave this room, I'd never turn back. And I knew I wanted to be part of something special. To change the world for the better. I never accomplished that goal, kid. At least, not the way I aspired to. But years passed and my aspirations changed. Not sure if it was memories of my childhood—my family being consistently broke and in debt. Maybe it was simply a sign of the times—Reaganomics and such. But the Sirens sang their songs of making money. Making money with no remorse for how it was made. What can I say? I was hooked. And then one day, I thought to myself, *You know what? This market—the way I can get that stack of cash to grow—that's special enough for me*. My moral compass may have been knocked off-kilter somewhere along the way, but who am I to judge? Mother nature *never* judges. She just persists…. Look, I love what I do. So I do it. The rush. The gratification."

"Do you ever feel guilty?"

"Sometimes. And when I do, I squash the guilt like a bug. Till it's dead on the bottom of my shoe. That's me. What about you, kid?"

Fifteen

Champ's father, Silvio, lay in a hospital bed with tubes running out of his nose and arm. He was forty-nine, but came across as weak as a geriatrics patient. For Champ, this was a sad and sobering sight.

A nurse came in, lifted Silvio's hairless head, fluffed his pillow, and left.

"If it isn't my beautiful boy," Silvio said softly. "The People's Champ. How are ya, pal?"

"Fine."

Silvio looked at a chair, inviting his son to sit down. "How are your classes going?"

Champ, preferring to stand, didn't respond.

"What's the matter? Cat got your tongue 'cause your Pops is a little sickly?"

"I guess I don't wanna talk about school."

"What, then?"

There was another awkward silence.

"I still can't believe you're working with Ira," Silvio said. "Who would've thought? Life's funny. He must've really identified with you. And yes, he has a checkered past, but that's the wonderful thing about this country. If you're lucky, you can get a second shot."

"What about *your* second shot?" Champ said gloomily. "*You* don't get one?"

He couldn't help noticing the imperfections in the room. A brown water-stained corner of the ceiling. A light film of dust on the windows overlooking the parking lot. Also, a tray to his father's side with a nearly untouched cup of chicken noodle soup and a bottle of Ensure.

"I don't want you to go, Pops. Not here. Not like this."

"Me, either. But I already know."

"Know what?"

"No matter how I go or where I go, I ain't scared."

"You honestly ain't scared?"

"C'mon, son. You've heard the cliché: Where I'm headed, there's no pain. I get to rest in peace. That's not so bad, right?"

"Right."

"No feeding tubes or colostomy bags. No nasty chemo drugs."

Champ hugged his ailing father.

"I have no regrets," Silvio said. "I love the life I was given."

"The life you *made*."

"The life I made." He pinched Champ's cheek. "*And* the boy I made."

"Sorry to interrupt," the nurse said, after clearing her throat. She quickly and quietly checked the machines around the bed and stepped out.

"My time's almost up, Champ," his father said weakly. "And I know I don't have much to leave you. These medical bills crushed me even *with* the insurance. They're probably gonna take the restaurant. I'm sorry, bud."

"What happened to no regrets? It's okay, Pops. I'm not a restaurateur anyway. You know this."

"Your mother would be very, very proud of you. Keep with the schoolwork. Don't stop, even after *I* stop. Promise me."

"I promise."

Again, the nurse barged in. "I apologize, cutie," she said. "Your dad needs his sleep, and visiting hours have ended."

Champ kissed his pale father on the forehead and said, "I love you."

"I love you, too." As his son headed out of the hospital room, Silvio added, "Be good, Champ."

"I will."

"Not *too* good. You'll—"

"Never have any fun. I know. Get some rest, Pops."

Sixteen

Parked on West 125th Street, Ira sipped 21-year-old scotch from the back of his Escalade. He had just left a meeting with Bill Clinton at the former president's office, located on the top floor of a high-rise building in Harlem. They had leisurely snacked on smoked Gouda and crackers, while discussing a variety of topics. From saxophones to sports. From trials and tribulations they had both suffered in their illustrious careers to their personal philosophies about the ever-growing connected global market. Although they disagreed with each other a fair amount, there was also a mutual affection.

"Downtown, sir?" Jerry the driver asked. His cologne permeated the entire car, but that didn't bother Ira. "Sir?"

"Yes," Ira said, perspiring. The wool suit he had on did not breathe well, causing him to take out an orange pocket square and wipe his forehead. "Hey, Jerry."

"Yes?"

"I change my mind. Take me to a hundred and ninth, between Madison and Fifth."

"El Barrio?"

"Let's make moves, Jerry. Chop chop!"

When they arrived, Ira rolled down the window and looked at an unadorned red-bricked church. Smashed up beside it stood a two-story building with a wheelchair ramp in front. A group of elderly men with canes were loitering under a sign that read:

NEW YORK'S
SOLICITOUS
PANTRY
SOLUTIONS FOR ALL SEASONS

"Sir?"

"Let's get outta here, Jerry. I'm ready."

"Ira?" a woman shouted. She dropped a trash bag next to the others on the side of the building. "Ira? It couldn't be."

"Sir? Should we go?"

"Hold on," Ira replied timidly. "Hold on."

The plump Puerto Rican approached the SUV. She didn't have on any makeup, exposing the fine lines on her cheeks and black under her eyes. "*Ay, dios mio*," she said. "It *is* you!"

Ira was rarely at a loss for words.

"Well, well," the woman said, leaning into the window. "Things are going okay, I see."

"Hi, Gloria."

"*Hola*, Ira," Gloria said with a wide grin. "Come inside and tell me all about what's been going on with you."

"I can't," Ira said. "I… I have meetings."

"Come, Ira," she insisted. "Come inside for a coffee and talk to me. I wanna know."

"Jerry, I'll be back shortly. Keep the engine running."

Ira got out and followed Gloria's round rump into the food shelter.

The two sat in a supply room to get some privacy.

"Tell me," Gloria implored.

"It's been a remarkable ride for me these last few months." Ira scratched his neck. "Remarkable."

"I can see that," Gloria said. "When I last saw you, you were still living day-to-day with your blind friend—"

"Tommy Boy."

Ira grabbed a can of tomato paste off a shelf and nervously fiddled with it in his clammy hands.

"So, tell me what's happened since."

"I was offered another chance," Ira explained. "Another chance at life. At greatness. To be the best I can be at what I do." He didn't dare look at Gloria. "I have a job at M and J Savings, where they pay me an offensive amount of money. A huge loft in Tribeca next to where the stars live. A driver who takes me wherever, whenever."

"And an amazing lady, hopefully?" Gloria asked, placing her hand on top of his.

"Lad*ies*," he answered. "That suffices for the time being."

"You look great," she said, removing her hand. "Still a bit foggy behind the eyes, but I mean, you look handsome."

"I wasn't handsome before?"

"You know what I'm trying to say, silly. You look clean and well kept. I mean…, it's… it's like you were a caterpillar. And now—"

"A butterfly. Thanks."

"I was pretty stunned when I caught you in that big black Cadillac. Was I ever, boy!"

Ira said nothing.

"So, what brought you to East Harlem from your castle downtown?" she asked.

"You won't believe me if I tell you."

"Try me."

"I was having cheese and crackers with Bill Clinton."

"Bullshit!"

"I shit you not."

"Lord!" she yelled. "I'll be damned. You *are* Mister Bigshot again!"

"I told ya," Ira said, letting out a smirk.

"That still doesn't explain what brought you *here*."

"I… for old time's sake. Since I was somewhat in the area, I figured—"

"You figured, since the pantry helped feed you once upon a time, you wanna help the pantry feed someone else?"

Ira knew this was a rhetorical question.

"Look at all these cans of food we're sitting on," Gloria said. "And these boxes. You know the drill. We get more and more families comin' in every day."

"I know."

"So you came by the kitchen to help out? Why else?" Gloria extended her hand to Ira. "Come."

Ira trailed behind her into the kitchen, where volunteers were busy keeping track of food bubbling in tall stockpots.

As she always did, Gloria quickly checked the stove for anything burning.

"Fernando!" she called to the man who was dishing out meals at the cafeteria-like counter.

"Yes, ma'am?"

"Take a break, honey. Our old friend here wants to take a crack at it."

Fernando rested a large serving spoon on the counter. "Hello," he said, pulling off his rubber gloves.

Ira set his suit jacket to the side, flung his tie over his shoulder, rinsed his hands, and put on a hairnet.

"The gloves are right there," Gloria said to Ira, pointing to the countertop. "They're waiting, sweetie. *Vamos*."

With a fresh pair of gloves, Ira went to work serving the struggling New Yorkers. Most of them were grateful and kind to him, just longing for somebody to talk to. Some didn't say a word. Some had toothless smiles or a screw loose up top, but they were like anyone else— simply wanting the basics. Food. Shelter. Clothing. Security. Stability. Dignity. Ira knew this as well as anyone. He remembered being on the other side of this same counter, eager to be served. He also remembered how they would let him shower and sometimes do laundry there.

$

A couple of hours later, Gloria returned to the windowless fluorescent-lit room where the homeless were filling their bellies.

"Ira, *como estás*? I think your shift's finished."

Ira wiped his brow and took off his hairnet and rubber gloves.

$

"How was it, huh?" Gloria asked, back outside in front of Ira's SUV.

"The place is exactly how I remember it."

"That's a compliment, I hope."

"It's incredible what you do here. That's all there is to it."

"It's not incredible, Ira. We're not superheroes, for god's sake. We're ordinary people, doing much-needed work. Trying to pay it forward, ya know?"

"You're doing amazing work. You're a saint."

"Pop by anytime. We always need more hands on deck. And you never know, god might be in the search for another saint to add to the list."

"You know, Gloria, I'm not sure what made me come by here today. I mean, I was afraid to see you, but—"

"Afraid?" she asked, surprised, almost angry. "Why's that?"

Ira lowered his head.

"Why?" she repeated.

"Because of the dubious choices I've made. The selfishness. But you... you represent the best in all of us—the human spirit. You're the best we got. You give and you give, and for what?"

"It might be more selfish than you think, Ira."

"How so?"

"Peace of mind. That's what I get. Peace of mind. In many ways, we do what makes us feel good inside, right? That's what does it for me. Helping those less fortunate. What can I say?"

Ira shook his head. "You saw me at my lowest. Strung out. Miserable and pathetic. A wretched soul. You didn't only feed me. You gave me a piece of your day. To listen. To care. You didn't judge me. You lent me an ear. You lent me your heart, and I will never, *ever* forget."

Gloria blinked, triggering a tear that ran down her cheek.

"And I want you to know I'm sorry I tried to kiss you that one time way back when. I needed—"

"Oh, stop it, Ira," she said wiping away the tear. "Water under the bridge. I know how it goes. People tend to get horny when lonely."

"Ha! Yeah. I guess that's true."

"I'm happy you're up on your feet. I'm proud of you."

"Thanks."

"Are *you* happy?" Gloria asked. "Are you at least *happier* now that you're back in the saddle?"

Ira knocked on the window to signal his driver. "Depends what day you ask me."

Instantly, Jerry popped out of the Escalade and opened the door for his boss. "Sir," he said.

"Come back," Gloria half-pleaded. "Come and help us again. We need it."

Ira pushed the lump down his throat before stepping into his ride. "I'll try, Gloria. I'll try."

"Don't *try*. Do. Come back and lighten that heavy heart of yours."

"I'll never forget," Ira said, as Jerry shut the rear door.

"*Adiós*," she replied.

Seventeen

On a cool April evening at the beach in Coney Island, Champ sat on a blanket next to Althea, who, like always, was exuding a calm, comfortable vibe. Sitting next to them were Tyler and Reese, rambunctiously clowning with each other.

"Shhh! Simmer down," Champ said. "Simmer. We can't be too loud. They patrol the sand on four-wheelers."

"Can I see the vapor pen?" Althea asked.

Champ handed her his G Pen and watched as she puffed away.

"Enough wax," Tyler said, waving a dime bag with a rocket pattern on it. "This is why we're here. Dimethyltryptamine."

"Here's the blindfolds," Reese said as he pulled two handkerchiefs from his back pocket.

Meanwhile, Tyler packed the DMT into a small glass pipe. "You lovebirds first," he said.

Champ looked to Althea.

"What?" she asked.

"I know I'm a lil' crazy," Champ said. "You don't have to do this if you don't want to."

"I'm attracted to two things," Althea said as a matter of fact. "Intelligence and a *little* crazy."

"A lil' crazy… all the time," Champ added, as if it were his personal motto.

Filled to the brim with confidence, Althea said, "Let's do it!"

After Reese blindfolded Champ and Althea, Tyler passed Champ the pipe and lit it for him. Champ, bursting with anticipation, held the hit in as long as he could, while Tyler helped Althea smoke next. Then the two exhaled simultaneously.

As if blasted out of a cannon traveling faster than the speed of sound, Champ was propelled far from Coney Island. Soon his ears perceived an undeniable low hum. Incredibly vivid visions strongly resembling ancient Tibetan tapestries appeared uninvited, overlapped, and faded away to nothing. Champ's third eye was mesmerized by mandalas.

Where did they come from and where were they going? He might have thought that, but couldn't be sure.

When the tapestries closed in on him and were seemingly in hand's reach, he attempted to grab them, but they washed over his hands like water with no beginning or end. There was no time. There was no beach. There was no him. There was *something*, though. Even blindfolded, Champ could see an alien-like figure in front of him. Perhaps an elf. It spoke using incomprehensible words and rhythms. Eventually, Champ's brain began to make out the words.

"Champ!" Tyler said. "Yo. You there? Champ!"

Reese untied the blindfolds. "So? How was it?" he asked.

Champ and Althea looked at each other and giggled.

"That good, huh?" Tyler said.

"Our turn, Ty!" Reese said excitedly.

Althea blindfolded Tyler and Reese, and Champ helped them each get a hit from the pipe. The whole high lasted ten to twenty minutes, but that was all they needed.

$

At daybreak, from the mighty east, the sun rose over the Atlantic.

"How picturesque," Althea said, holding a shark eye shell she had dug up earlier in the sand. "Look at that sunrise. So inspiring. A perfect beginning to a perfect day. We're blessed."

"Yeah," Champ replied. "We are."

"I know I didn't get to meet him, but I'm sorry about your father," she said, uncertain if it were the appropriate time to do so. "From the stories you told me, he sounded like a sweet man."

"Yeah," Tyler said as he lay on his back. "I'm gonna miss him."

"Me, too," Reese said. "He was the coolest dad in the neighborhood."

"Except that time he caught us throwing a party at the restaurant in the middle of the night, and tried to beat our asses," Tyler said.

"He kept chasing us," Champ recalled. "But he was too slow."

"Then he tripped on that chair and wiped out, face first, on the carpet," Reese said, smiling. "He was fuming, yo. I thought he was gonna straight choke us out."

Together they all enjoyed a cathartic laugh.

"To Silvio! Rest in peace," Tyler said, putting out his hand in the middle of the group.

The other three stacked their hands on top of his.

"To Silvio!" they cheered in unison.

Eighteen

"The OCC's all up in my goddamn poopshoot," Ira said, after reading his computer screen. He sipped bourbon on the rocks as he looked out over the southern tip of the island.

"OCC?" Champ asked, standing by the door.

"C'mon, kid. Aren't ya doin' your homework? The Office of Comptroller of the Currency."

"What about them?" Champ asked. He smirked. "How are they all up in your... shoot?"

Ira read an excerpt of an article from the *Huffington Post*: "The identified issues include a massive backlog of thousands of alerts, identifying suspicious activity that has yet to be reviewed, ineffective methods for identifying suspicious activity, and a failure to file timely Suspicious Activity Reports with U.S. law enforcement."

"Sounds like a pretty scathing report," Champ said.

"Yeah. Suddenly they care what M and J's doing? What an act. This government of ours is a fickle bitch. All slobberin' on your dick one day, and kickin' you in the nuts the next. Whichever fits their agenda. Essentially standing for nothin'."

"Are we at risk of getting in trouble? I can't—"

"No worries, kid. It's my job to stay three steps ahead of these fascists who are trying to tell us how to make money."

"Now it's you versus the fascists on Capitol Hill?" Champ asked sarcastically.

Ira finished what was left of his whiskey. "I was made for this game. They almost got me once. *Almost* being the key word. They couldn't make it stick. I'm even stronger and sharper, the second time around."

"Could you be a tiny bit cautious, please?" Champ asked. "For both our sakes."

"Hey," Ira said as he poured another round of Woodford Reserve Master's Collection. "The more room they give me, the more I take. That's how empires are built. It's human nature to carry out the dream *or* the scheme as far as it'll go. To the absolute limit. Until someone or something finally says, 'Enough. You can unequivocally go no further.' Understand? Until that day, you keep pressing to get to the pot of gold at the end of the rainbow. In other words, sometimes having a pair rules over having intelligence."

"Having a pair?"

"Balls, kid! Gonads. The size of melons. Yeah, I got a head on my shoulders, Champ, and that's great. But more importantly, I'm sure as hell always willing to push the envelope and see what happens. That's the secret to success in this business. Maybe *every* business. Ego. Balls over brains. Besides, the odds are greatly in our favor."

"What odds?"

"Have a seat."

Champ sat on the other side of Ira's imposing mahogany desk.

"A few crack rocks can get a young punk from the hood jail time," Ira stated. "Rikers. For who knows how long? Right? This—" Ira pointed to his computer screen. "This doesn't put people in prison. Not people like us. We're white. And we work for a financial institution. A prestigious one, at that. Banks pay fines. Who cares? M and J certainly doesn't. We keep on plowing ahead—making profits."

"May I?" Champ asked, referring to the Kentucky spirit.

"Ice?"

"Neat."

Ira filled a lowball glass and slid it across the desk. "By the way," he said, "I wanna change the subject for a minute. I'm sorry about your Pops. I sincerely am. Anything you need, you can ask me. Anything. *Capisce?*"

"*Capisce*," Champ said.

"I already worked it out with Silvio—your tuition bills. It was his one request, if I could help, and I can. So I will. Like I told ya, you can shack with me in Tribeca. I keep it interesting, don't I?"

"Definitely."

"We can run amok together in this town. You got the looks, and I got the dough. We'll be swimmin' in muff."

"Thanks. I appreciate it. But I think I'll stay with my buddies in the Village. And I've told you before, I'm seeing someone. We're kinda serious."

"Serious?" Ira scoffed. "You're too young for *serious*. You should be cumming in every nook and cranny of this city, not settling down. That's the *last* thing you should be doing."

Champ didn't agree or disagree.

"No," Ira continued. "I can appreciate tender puppy love. I'm sure you two are adorable. Sharing a sundae at an ice cream parlor. Strolling through the park hand-in-hand. Am I wrong?"

"C'mon, man."

"Getting a tug job at the movie theater under a jacket," Ira added, making a jerking motion with his hand.

"How young do you think I am?"

"I at least want your address," Ira said. "I wanna know where you're resting your head at night, okay? And remember—my place—it's an open invitation."

"Thanks. I appreciate it."

"Let's have a toast." Ira held his glass in the air.

"For what?"

"To your future, kid. Your future. May it be exhilarating, prosperous, and full of pussy!"

The two toasted and drank fine bourbon.

"Listen, Champ," Ira said, concluding their prior conversation as he kicked his patent leather shoes onto his desk, "banks protect their own. They aren't quick to throw their high-level employees under the bus. Because once you reach a certain level in this biz, it's us versus them. We look out for *us*. So, for the most part, places akin to M and J have their employees avoid criminal charges. Shit, man. Prosecutions for bank fraud are the lowest they've been in the last two decades. You can thank your chosen one, Obama, for that. So, that's it."

"That's it, huh?" Champ said skeptically, taking another sip.

"We're doin' good. Record earnings. CEO bonus checks. Facts are facts, kid. Bringing me back to my ingenious plan."

"Which is?"

"We march on. We march on because the OCC *knows* what we're doing. Not the full scale of what we're doing, but they're not oblivious, either. And I know what they're gonna do."

"What's that?"

"Give us a slap on the wrist. Fine M and J a fraction of what it makes, and call it a day. After a short time, it'll all be forgotten, and we'll make record profits again till the *next* slap on the wrist. It's a cyclical thing. We'll be alright."

Champ sighed. "So why does it feel so sketchy?"

Nineteen

Thinking they were being discreet, Champ and his two best friends puffed a joint on a stoop at the corner of 59th and Third. Besides the jay, they guzzled down Gansett tall boys.

"Whose turn?" Tyler asked, pulling out a few whippets and a metal cracker with a punch balloon attached.

"Me," said Champ.

After the balloon was filled to capacity, he dumped the used cartridges on the ground and sucked until it was deflated.

"Your lips are turning blue," Reese told his buddy as he fiendishly snatched the cracker from him. "My turn."

When the box of cartridges was empty, the boys jumped on their decks and finished their game of S.K.A.T.E.

"Hey!" Champ kicked his board into his hand as they reached 68th and Lex. "I got class."

"Ha!" Reese said. "Stop it, man. C'mon, let's head uptown. There's this nasty stairwell I wanna show you guys."

"Yeah," Tyler agreed. "I'm down."

"Nah," Champ said, pointing. "My class is right there. I'm gonna go."

"Goin' to class all wasted?" Reese said, dogging his pal. "I just saw you spewing chunks all over the fucking corner."

"Shame, shame," Tyler added. "*And* you barely had any z's last night. We were out late as fuck."

"No books, either?" Reese asked.

"Eh, fuck it." Champ shrugged. "I'm almost done with this class anyway. But I gotta show—for my attendance count."

"Control fraud," Professor Laurence was declaring as Champ tried to slip in unnoticed twenty minutes into the lecture. Disapproving, the professor shook his head, but continued on. "William K. Black coined the term. He said it is when a trusted person in a high position of responsibility subverts an organization by engaging in extensive fraud for personal gain. Not such a shocking premise. Not such an astonishing conspiracy."

All eyes were on the professor. All but Champ's. Incredibly, his were already closed, with his head propped up on Althea's shoulder.

"In fact," Professor Laurence added, "it happens every day and everywhere. So, please don't go out there in the real world as ignorant adults. Blind to the ways of mankind. Ignorance is bliss. That may be true, but knowledge is power, people." He let this last sentence sink in. "Now, *mes enfants*, the Savings and Loan Crisis of the 1980s. Shall we talk about that? We know from our reading assignments there were various causes of the crisis. Today, we'll try to focus in on a couple of those. Causes of greed and deceit without protection from our federal government. First, someone remind me what a savings and loan association does."

In the front row, a hipster-looking type with a handlebar mustachio enthusiastically raised his hand in a heartbeat.

The professor nodded. "Erik, take it away."

"An S and L," said Erik, "takes its depositors' investments and puts them mainly into residential mortgage loans. Also, some commercial real estate and consumer loans."

"That's correct, Erik," the professor said. "Now let's travel back in time about thirty years. The 1980s.

Big hair and big money. Under the Carter and Reagan administrations, regulations on S and L's were all but stripped away as a supposed attempt to balance the scales for impediments like higher interest rates, which affected the S and L's and their depositors' revenues. Keep it going. Erik?"

"The way I understand it, thousands of S and L's were giving massive amounts of loans with virtually no oversight by the government. Many of the loans were speculative and overly risky."

"Yes," the professor agreed. "The risk was partially justified because the depositors' investments were supposed to be insured by an institution called the Federal Savings and Loans Insurance Company, or FSLIC for short. Keep going, Erik."

"Without proper regulation, bad loan after bad loan defaulted at an extremely high rate. But the S and L's kept granting loans, making poor decisions as they spent more than they made."

"*Oui*!" Professor Laurence shouted. "Many of those thrifts were *hemorrhaging* money! Now, what, my dear students, did all this hemorrhaging lead to? Jennifer?"

"Ponzi schemes?" the Korean girl with cat-eye glasses said.

"Say it as though you mean it, love," said the professor. "And why did it lead to Ponzis? Champ!"

Champ woke from his slumber, embarrassed that he was startled. "I have no fuckin' clue," he said obnoxiously with his eyelids hung low.

The class erupted with laughter, except for the professor and Althea.

"After class, my office," Professor Laurence said to Champ. "The rest of you settle down. *Calmez-vous.* Don't encourage idiocy. Ponzi schemes. Althea, care to enlighten your friend why there was an influx?"

"They basically lied their asses off, so as not to go insolvent, and pretended that they were still making monstrous profits."

"Insolvency." The professor thought about the answer. "Wait…. Those titans of industry…, business graduates from the most prestigious universities…, they simply *lied their asses off*, as Althea so eloquently put it?"

The class giggled.

"Cooked the books like some Mafia pizzeria in Nutley, New Jersey?" the professor added. "Fooled their investors and acted as if it would all be hunky-dory? That's *all* these cretins did?" He took a few seconds for effect. "Many with the protection of paid-off congressmen and other officials. That brings me to my original concept of the day. Control fraud. The way this crisis we're currently discussing was able to function and then implode similarly to a massive star under its own gravitational pressure. Control fraud was the grease that allowed the wheels to spin with ease, my students. Whether being paid to lobby for looser laws or misleading unqualified investors, this was about rich men trying to get richer at *any* cost. *Control fraud.* Let's open our texts to page four hundred and seventy-seven and continue our dialogue. We'll delve into the FSLIC's incapability to insure those bad loans and the subsequent bailout by the nation's taxpayers. Did we learn our lesson after that financial crisis, or have we been doomed to repeat our mistakes over and over again?" The professor let his students contemplate the question for a brief moment. "Finals are around the corner. Let's read. We must push on to the bitter end."

$

After class, Champ sat in Professor Laurence's tidy office with his hood on his head and his face cradled in his hands.

The professor walked in with a hot cup of coffee, and placed it on the corner of his desk closest to Champ. "Drink this," he said as he sat in his chair.

Champ took a sip.

"What's *this* all about? Huh?" the professor asked, pointing at his weary student.

"I didn't get enough sleep last night." Champ rubbed his eyes. "I was studying."

"Bullshit! Don't fib me, boy. I don't have time for that. I have another class in fifteen minutes."

"I had a beer before class. Okay?"

"A very *tall* beer, I presume." Professor Laurence sniffed in his student's direction. "And you reek like bush weed, man. You think I have time to waste on someone who can't show me the least bit of common courtesy? Half-asleep on your new squeeze."

"It won't happen again, Professor Laurence. I swear."

"No, it won't." The professor glared at Champ uncomfortably. "I looked into that Mister Mace of yours. Did some investigating. He's a gem, that Mister Mace. A master manipulator. A sorcerer who conjures up moneymaking magic."

"Professor, I know he—"

"Magic tricks are illusions, Champ. Nothing tangible. Numbers floating from one account to another. In the end, when gluttonous corporations like M and J cannibalistically eat themselves from the inside out until there is nothing left to feast on, who pays the price? M and J? I think not. It's *us*. The taxpayers. And who must come swooping in to the rescue, for some inexplicable reason, to resuscitate those lawbreaking villains? It's *us*. The taxpayers."

Champ worked on his coffee without replying.

"I see what you're thinking over there," said the professor. "I see. You want to say it, but you won't. You're thinking to yourself, *Hey, you teach a goddamn economics class — getting students ready to work for those companies, you hypocrite!* Am I close? Huh?"

Champ looked away.

"Ahh! I *am* close." Professor Laurence leaned back in his chair. "Our time together is ending shortly. Your exams are in less than a week."

"Hallelujah," Champ muttered.

"Perhaps there will be a day when you will respect what I teach. I teach the harsh truth so that maybe a small percent — that ten out of a hundred rolling through my doors — can go against the grain and do things the honest way. The *right* way. Now, what I *do* need you to understand is this school has strict policies regarding being intoxicated during our lectures. Understood?"

"Yes, sir," Champ said obediently, standing to leave.

"You know, son, that clever mentor of yours, Mister Mace, reminds me of an old proverb from Cameroon, my home country. Translated into English, the proverb says: Every smart man is an ignoramus who flaunts his own ignorance. See you in class on Thursday."

Twenty

Ira checked his Rolex. It was 9:00 P.M. on the dot. A large, muscular Polynesian opened the door to 13F. His tuxedo was undersized for his bulging physique, and his jet-black hair formed a braided tail in the back. Ira was wearing a tuxedo as well, with a red flower in the chest pocket. He tried to peer behind the Polynesian, but couldn't see anything.

"Can I help you?" the massive man asked. He had a mean mug and an earpiece tucked in his canal.

"Aurum," Ira replied.

"Come with me, sir." The Polynesian relaxed his furrowed brow, led Ira down a corridor to a soundproof wooden door, and said, "You may enter."

As Ira walked into a grand ballroom, he could hear the suction of the door as it sealed shut behind him. The room's decor was made to appear like something out of the eighteenth century—reminiscent of an after-hours party hosted by King George III. An extravagant affair. No corners were cut, and no expenses were spared to get the decadence just so.

At the far end, an elegant man doing his best to look and sound like Mozart was playing an antique Viennese piano. Ira noticed a dozen other men in the room, all in tuxedos. Most of them, clearly familiar with each other, were chatting away on lavish couches, while wearing Zanni masquerade masks that covered the top half of their faces and had elongated phallic noses. A few guests, however, like Ira, were not wearing masks.

Hanging above him was a fancy banner that read:

HELFIER

Fais ce que tu voudras

"Hellfire," said a man whose mask had Indian feathers shooting out. Unlike any of the other tuxedos, his was bright white.

"It took me a second, but I got it," said Ira.

"What do you think so far?" the man in white asked.

"Not sure yet."

The masked man clapped twice. "Let's get a stiff drink in your hand this instant!"

A barmaid appeared out of nowhere, wearing a drab brown dress with an attached white apron and matching bonnet.

"How may I serve you tonight, sire?" she asked.

"Gin and tonic," Ira said.

"Of course, sire." The barmaid bowed like a lady and scurried away.

"Who are you?" Ira asked the man.

"You can call me Chief White Cloud."

"Why's that?"

"A portion, albeit a slim portion, of my American lineage precedes the *Mayflower* itself—going back to the natives of this land. I'll be your host for the evening, so let me know if there's anything you desire."

The barmaid returned with the gin and tonic, bowed again, and went off to take more orders.

"You must be elated," the host said.

"Elated?"

"Yes. Elated. To be invited."

"Fuck, I don't even know why I'm here." Ira gulped down his drink.

White Cloud clapped his hands twice and proclaimed, "Our guest needs another gin and tonic, please! This time, go heavier on the Nolet's!"

"What exactly was I invited *to*?" Ira asked. "Is this like Skull and Bones? Lying in coffins? Animal sacrifices? Pentagrams drawn in blood? Huh? Because I'll tell ya, I'm not into that kinda shit."

"Ha! In blood," White Cloud repeated uneasily. "Very amusing. No, no, no. We don't do those kinds of rituals here. We prefer *another* sin."

Instantly, the barmaid hurried over with Ira's glass and traded it for his empty one. She bowed and was off to another group of men.

"So, tell me," Ira said. "What kind of sin *does* take place in this private palace?"

"The sin of pleasure." White Cloud clapped twice once more. "Gentlemen! It's time!" He turned to Ira. "This particular gathering is my humble *homage* to Ben Franklin and his mysterious… *meetings*, shall we say…, with the elite of England, two hundred and fifty years ago to the day."

"I see," said Ira. "And what's this pleasure you mentioned earlier, huh? What do you have in—?"

"Ah, here they come!" White Cloud interrupted as he looked across the room.

What appeared to be a bookcase, but was actually a hidden door, opened, revealing a secret passageway.

All the men instantly perked up as a stream of women wearing panniers, corsets, and silk gowns that showed off plenty of cleavage filed out from behind the hidden door and into the ballroom. Their faces were caked with powdered makeup. Feminine Colombina masks covered their eyes, and white wigs were piled high on their heads. Immediately and shamelessly, they rushed the men and flirted with them by sitting on their laps or tugging at their flies and giggling.

Ira stared intently at the women, licking his chops. When he turned to his host, the man with the feathered mask was gone. In his place was one of the voluptuous harlots.

"Will you come with me, sire?" she asked, taking his arm.

"No small talk? No foreplay?"

"But why?" she asked.

Ira followed her past the piano player, through the hidden door. She led him by the hand up a narrow staircase, while his other hand held his gin.

They entered a plush bedroom lit by a Tiffany lamp. A woman was sitting patiently on a bed covered with satin sheets. Unlike the others, she was wearing a modern black backless dress and a gold Bauta mask that was beautifully ornate with a strong square jaw. Her wild curly red hair fell to her shoulders.

The harlot looked seductively at Ira, bowed like a lady, and left the room.

"Are you enjoying yourself?" the woman in the gold mask asked Ira. "Enticed?"

"I'm intrigued. Though, I'm still learning. What happens next?"

"I think you can guess. Can't you?" She slithered closer to him.

"I have intuition. Yes."

"Intuition," whispered the redhead. "And also, big balls. Not literally, of course. Or maybe you do?"

"Do I know you?"

"I'm the one who invited you here in the first place."

"Catherine?" Ira whispered, as if trying to keep a secret. "Are you one of the whores?"

"Me? A whore? Don't be ridiculous! This isn't purely a boy's club anymore! Idiot! How dare you! *I* choose who gets in this bed! Who eats this pussy! Don't forget it!"

"What do you want from *me*?" Ira asked.

"I want us to bond. A rare time for us to join together and be our primal selves. I want to feel your… *energy* deep inside me. That's what I want from you." She clapped twice.

"Madam?" the young tramp said on being summoned back into the bedroom. "Should I start undressing him?"

"Yes."

With her dress intact, the woman in the gold mask was soon riding Ira hard, as the harlot, now topless, played with herself and passionately kissed Ira's neck.

Ira couldn't help suspecting he was being watched. Possibly by a hidden camera.

Evidence that could be used to blackmail me later? he thought. *Am I just another whore in this room?*

The woman in the gold mask let out a moan as Ira clamped down on her hips.

Don't forget, Ms. Finer, I'm no rube, he thought. *I'm not a servant wrapped around your pinky. I choose who rides this dick.*

Twenty-One

Somewhere in the outskirts of Sayulita, Ira and Champ were being driven to one of Mr. Manny's many estates, nestled in a tropical forest. Once beyond the heavily guarded gate, they saw a pair of gunmen standing by the front door. The goons greeted them with a not-so-friendly pat-down and confiscated their phones. Then the duo was escorted inside.

From the foyer, the open floor plan allowed them to see Mr. Manny and some of his closest confidants chewing the fat far away in the living room. Ira noticed a common theme in their look. Slicked back hair. Pastel-colored short sleeve button-downs. And amber-tinted metal frame glasses.

"Welcome back below the border," Mr. Manny said in a charming Spanish accent. He was sitting on a bright white L-shaped couch, while his men stood behind him.

"Thank you," Ira replied. "It's a pleasure to finally meet you in the flesh."

"Yes, yes. And I you, Mister Mace."

"Call me Ira. And this is Champ."

"Why the boy?"

"He helps me get by. He's a good guy. On the level."

"Not *too* on the level, I hope."

They shared a quick laugh.

"Come. Sit with me. Drink? Water? Something with more kick? I have a bottle of fine tequila that would have you orgasming right in your pants."

"No, we're fine. Thank you."

Ira and Champ sat in a couple of chairs that were facing the kingpin.

"So, enough small talk, then," Mr. Manny said. "My time's limited. What brings you to my home?"

"You truly carved out a thick slice of heaven here. You really outdid yourself."

"*Gracias, mi amigo.* What can I say? Life's good. *La vida es buena*! Now, tell me. I assume you didn't come all this way just to compliment my hacienda, did you?"

"We needed to discuss some business that I figured would be better handled in person."

"You couldn't take care of this with the Jew lawyer? Now you have me curious. What is this business we must discuss?"

"It has to do with all the deposits."

"Deposits?"

"Yes. Duffel bags and duffel bags of American dollars being deposited relentlessly at Banco Maya."

"And?"

"And, well, I'm hoping we can slow down for a second. I can't believe I'm sayin' this, but I think I underestimated you."

"Why would you do *this*? You know, I seem to recall Mister Lipschitz saying that you could take as much as we could give. 'We can take it all,' was exact quote, if I'm not mistaken."

"I just think…, we should take a step back and reassess the situation."

"Nonsense! Everything's been running smoothly. Easy."

"*Too* easy."

"*Too* easy? There's no such thing."

"The Justice Department has been sticking their nose in M and J's business more than usual, these past few weeks. I wouldn't want to give them a meatball to knock out of the park if I can avoid it."

"That sounds like a YP, not an MP, Ira. *Tu problema*. *No es mi problema*."

"That's where you're dead wrong, Mister Manny. I advise you to not be shortsighted at this point in time."

"I must ask you, Ira—what exactly do you *do* for me? How do I benefit from your services?"

"I can solve issues others don't wanna touch with a ten-foot pole."

"Like?"

"Like getting an overly confident drug general who leads an army of thugs to do what *I* say."

Arms akimbo, Mr. Manny's men seemed off-put from Ira's brazen comment, but soon, to their surprise, the head honcho was doubled over with laughter.

"*Este tipo esta loco!*" he exclaimed to his minions. "I like you, Ira Mace! I like you!"

"As I was saying," said Ira, "I think we should take a small step back…. Ya know—make certain everything's unflawed. Try to get a harness around this bucking bronco and tighten the reins some.

"So, you plan to tame the beast?" Mr. Manny asked, crossing his legs and folding his hands across his lap. "Is that it? There's no taming a beast, Ira. You should know that by now. You *feed* the beast. Give it what it wants so it doesn't… harm you."

"The tellers and managers at our subsidiary down here are accepting every cent you throw at them, out of fear."

"They're smart."

"Fear for their lives."

"They're *very* smart."

"I told Lipschitz no bullying. That's not how we do business."

"Really? I don't think the ways in which our businesses operate are so different from each other, Ira. Do you?"

"How so?"

"We both take what we want and apologize to no one."

Ira said nothing.

"Listen," Mr. Manny said, "we *need* each other. It's symbiosis. Tell me what you want from me, and I'll try to oblige. I'm a reasonable man... when I choose to be."

"A month!" Champ blurted out.

"What's that?" asked Mr. Manny.

"Give us a month," Champ said.

"One month to iron out any kinks and make certain everything is copacetic," Ira added. "Look, this is about making sure all of your accounts with M and J are safe and secure. Help me help you."

"One month," Mr. Manny agreed. "You get *one month*. But I must warn you, Ira—if you ask for more time—stunting my growth in any way, well..., you know. Champ..., you know?"

"Yes, sir."

"Boy, make sure you boss don't end up hurt,"

the man directly behind the drug lord said in broken English. "This no good."

"Don't fail me," Mr. Manny said. "I'm assuming you can find your way out."

Ira and Champ stood up, looking at each other uncomfortably, as one of Mr. Manny's crew whispered in his ear.

"Ah, yes," the boss said. "Where are my manners? I have a running tab with the best resort in Puerto Vallarta. It's magnificent. Why don't you two fly there in my plane and do some R and R."

"We would love to do that, Mister Manny, but we have to head back to New York to—"

"Nonsense! I *insist*. Kick back for a couple. My treat. So you can't ever say that I'm not a nice guy."

"Sure," Ira and Champ said over each other.

"Then, it's settled. You leave now. Enjoy and make sure you protect that pasty gringo skin."

$

Two days later, Ira and Champ were lying side-by-side on massage tables in Puerto Vallarta. They were being rubbed and pampered in a cozy cabana, while listening to CNN on a flat screen above the bar. Not twenty steps away, carefree vacationers were frolicking in the glistening ocean under the high July sun.

"Hopefully, we don't have to come down here again for a while," Ira said as a masseuse applied a Mayan clay facial mask.

"It ain't so bad here, boss," said Champ.

"I guess you're right, kid. I guess you're right. Besides, I would do about anything for this cash cow. Can you believe the amount of flow these guys have? It's mind-boggling."

"It is."

"Notwithstanding a few snags, we're doin' alright."

"Snags, huh? That's what you call 'em?"

"Snags, kid. Nothing too detrimental to the cause."

"They're aggressive," Champ said as he got his hamstrings and calves kneaded. "I don't know if you *can* slow them down. They're like a runaway locomotive."

"That's why they pay me the big bucks, kid. Let me explain something. Mister Manny may have countless bricks of coke and dope. He may have the arsenal of an army. He may have tunnels running under the border. But he'd be up shit's creek without a paddle if he didn't have a refined mind with giant *cojones* like I have. If not for me, he'd be buryin' a billion of blood money somewhere in the sweltering Mexican desert. This cartel is a bunch of savages. Let *them* do the killing. The extorting. The drug peddling. We'll keep skimming off the top and quietly reap the benefits. See?"

"Yeah."

"Nevertheless, we'll be on our way out *mañana*, and then it's back to the grind."

"Honestly, I would stay here for the rest of the week if it were my choice."

"Hell, no," Ira said. "You don't get vacation time yet."

"Fine, fine."

"This *would* be a great place for a refuge, I must admit. I'm tellin' ya. Welcoming locals. Good food. Fun in the sun."

"Maybe bring the family, one day," Champ said.

"Yeah, don't think that's in the cards for me. Ya know, I got two daughters."

"You do? I knew from your Wiki page you have an ex-wife, but—"

"They won't even speak to me. They haven't for almost their whole goddamn lives. Their cunt of a mother badmouthed me to no end and ruined any semblance of a relationship I ever had with them. Eventually, she got her talons on half my earnings, too. That vulture woman really did a number on me. That was many moons ago."

"Damn!"

"The saddest part is, I don't even know where they are—my daughters. Where they live."

"We could hire someone to—"

"Miss, please, the volume!" Ira sat up urgently with green clay spread all over his face. "*Sube el volumen*! *Por favor*!"

"Today," Wolf Blitzer was reporting on the TV, "marks the end of an era for Mexico's relentless drug trade. A U.S.-supported raid of the infamous Salazar cartel turned into a bloody massacre. According to our sources, the cartel's leader, Manuel Salazar, more commonly known as Mister Manny, and several of his top men have been shot dead by special forces who were ordered to return any hostile fire. More on this gory tale as additional information comes in, later in the program."

"Holy shit!" Champ was noticeably spooked by the news.

"Do you know what this means?" Ira said, joyfully. "Any idea what this fuckin' means?"

"I think it means we should get back to New York. Like, *now*!" Champ nervously wrapped a towel around his waist. As jumpy as he was, he was perplexed by his boss's devilish grin. "What should we do?"

"Go to the rooms and get our stuff while I call our pilot and make sure he's gassed up and ready," Ira said, eerily calm. He checked his Rolex. "Don't worry, kid. We'll be fine. Trust me."

Twenty-Two

"Love you," Althea said as she gently touched Champ's cheek and kissed him.

"I love you, too," Champ said after they unlocked lips.

Enjoying a relaxing summer day in the middle of Central Park, the couple was sitting on a bench as diehard roller skaters danced on the blacktop in front of them. Disco classics were playing from an old boom box with a broken antenna.

"Isn't this fun?" Althea said. "When we come here?"

"It's a lil' weird," Champ said sheepishly. His skateboard was resting upright against his leg. "But, yeah, I can dig it."

"Good." Althea kissed her man again on the lips under the tree swallows serenading each other on the branches above. "How's work going with you? Anything new?"

"I don't wanna talk about work," Champ said dismissively. "It's boring."

"Boring? Please. Or could it be you don't *ever* wanna talk to me about work? Your mysterious exploits with Mister Mace."

"Maybe."

"C'mon. Tell me *something*. And I don't need specifics. I wanna know about *you*. How *you're* feeling. Lately, you've been distant. You can tell me, Champ. You can tell me anything."

"Something feels off, I guess."

"Off?"

"I've been thinking about right and wrong a lot lately."

"What about right and wrong?"

"I mean, are they manmade concepts? Not real?"

"What do you mean?"

"Right and wrong seem to be relative to who's judging. Like beauty, it seems to be in the eye of the beholder."

"I suppose."

"These Fortune 500 companies." Champ shook his head. "It's the American way—the way of the world— to make money at any cost."

"Is that right or wrong?" Althea asked.

"Maybe it just *is*."

"So, you think a corporation has carte blanche to do whatever it pleases?"

"M and J's an institution—serving an important role in this country for nearly half a century. It's part of the lifeblood of this nation. Whatever it needs to do to be successful is ultimately worth it."

"Do you really believe that?"

"I don't know. But it's like… like what we do is… civilized? How could it be wrong?"

"Going to work in a designer suit doesn't make it civilized," she said.

"There's so much money to be made."

They briefly watched the roller skaters line up mini orange cones and start to weave through them.

"That's what it comes down to?" Althea asked. "You want the money?"

Champ made his answer clear by saying nothing.

"Isn't it wrong if it's made from stepping on the necks of others," Althea asked.

"It's what giant corporations do. Wouldn't most people step on a neck or two if it improved their situation? Let him who is without sin cast the first stone."

Althea rolled her eyes. "Bible quotes? Really?"

"I'm playing devil's advocate."

"Don't," she said. "Get honest."

"It's such a golden opportunity I'm being offered."

"I know."

"I can do what no one in my family was ever able to do—not have to worry. Not have to survive paycheck to paycheck. I could win. Win the game."

"What if it's not a game, Champ? Have you ever thought of that?"

"I'm baffled. I don't know what to think," he said.

"What's your gut say?"

Champ looked away.

"Remember our pinky swear?"

"I remember. Don't sell my soul to the almighty dollar."

"Good. Don't ever forget it, because you're my sweet boy. I *know* you are."

Althea smiled warmly and planted a wet one on Champ's neck. In her retro short shorts and brown roller skates with pink trim and pink wheels, she skated backwards toward the other quad-skaters and began getting her groove on to the funk coming from the radio.

Champ gave her a supportive thumbs-up. He was a fan of the show.

Starting with some basic heel rolls, Althea progressed into infinity rolls. Inside toe rolls. There were even a few side-to-side slides. The girl was on point.

Twenty-Three

Ira and Champ were sitting in the rear of a helicopter, aviation headsets on, soaring high above the Hudson River near lower Manhattan. An unknown man in a suit, black sunglasses, and black leather gloves was sitting between them.

Winslow, also wearing a headset, was facing front next to the pilot. "Gentlemen," he said. "You did a topnotch job with our Mexican constituents. Exceedingly profitable."

"We did," Ira said arrogantly. "I agree."

"You could imagine how disappointed we were," Winslow said, "to learn of the raids and subsequent demise of the Salazar cartel. Those men *did* live on the dangerous side. Didn't they, Champ?"

"Yes, sir."

"Easy come, easy go," Winslow said. "Yes, Mister Mace?"

"Who's this guy next to me, Winslow?" Ira asked. "And why is he breathing on my goddamn neck? Smells putrid. Like rotten hummus."

"Nonetheless," Winslow continued, ignoring Ira, "we did notice that dozens of accounts linked to the cartel were recently terminated. Poof. Where did it all go, Mister Mace? We're more than curious."

"Terminated accounts?" Ira said with a smirk.

"The board finds it less humorous," Winslow said. "We took a chance on you. So?"

"So?" Ira asked.

"Where the hell did it all go? We had our best men research the issue, and *no one* can seem to trace the funds or even tell us precisely how much is missing."

"Poof," Ira said mystically, as though he had just performed a magic trick.

"We at M and J do not tolerate behavior such as yours," Winslow said. "It's unacceptable. Understand me, Mister Mace? Unacceptable!"

"Stop speaking to me like a child, Grandpa," Ira said. "Besides, you still saw your cut of the lion's share. You all did. What's it to you what happened to the rest?"

"It wasn't yours!" Winslow shouted. He straightened his bow tie and then parted his white hair, attempting to calm himself. "You stole from *us*. From your employer."

"Please," Ira said. "That money belonged to a decimated drug cartel, not you."

"It wasn't yours to keep!"

"Then whose?"

"What you've done is unethical, to say the least."

"Unethical? *Unethical*? You got a lot of *chutzpah* mentioning ethics. I know your goddamn business. What you're about. It ain't roses, and it ain't daffodils."

Winslow gestured to the unknown man, who opened the door and shoved Ira over the edge until he was hanging halfway out of the chopper. The man's firm grip on Ira's coat was the only thing that prevented him from plummeting to his death.

"You *will* tell me where that money went!" Winslow said.

"I can't tell you shit if I'm splattered all along Battery Park, now, can I?" Ira yelled, thrashing about.

"Perhaps. Perhaps not."

Petrified, Champ froze up stiff as a mannequin.

With the wind whipping against his body, Ira watched as his wallet that had fallen from his pants pocket spiraled downward until it disappeared out of view.

"Let me point something out to you clear as day, Mister Mace. We talked about getting rid of you…, just so you understand. We entertained the idea of sending a professional to the place where you live to strangle the life right out of you. Ms. Finer somehow convinced us you're still worth more to us alive than dead. You can thank *her* for that. No more going rogue. None of that maverick horseshit! Understood?"

"Understood!" Ira shouted, still dangling half out of the helicopter.

"What was that?" asked Winslow.

"Understood!" Ira shouted at the top of his lungs. "Understood!"

"I think we should move ahead to future projects," Champ chimed in. "What's done is done. Easy come, easy go. Don't you agree, Mister Winslow? Should we move on?"

"Fine," Winslow said. "Future projects. Very well. But this isn't over."

He nodded to the unknown man, who yanked Ira back inside and closed the door.

"Our next issue," Winslow said, facing front again, "will be on the upcoming Nuisance Report, but I figured I would let you both in on it now, seeing that Mister Mace refuses to come to any board meetings, and the report doesn't come out until next Thursday."

Disheveled, Ira folded his arms, pouting like a scolded toddler.

"What's the issue?" Champ asked.

"Al Rajhi," Winslow said. "Champ, what do you know about Al Rajhi?"

"Al Rajhi is Saudi Arabia's largest private bank, owned by the Al Rajhi family. Assets top sixty billion dollars."

"Impressive, young man," Winslow said. "They're threatening to withdraw all their monies from M and J worldwide if our American branches don't comply with them. The problem is, our government's not allowing any of our American branches to work with Al Rajhi. Because of their *alleged* ties to terrorists."

"They were financing Osama bin Ladin, for crying out loud," Ira said.

Winslow didn't respond.

"What is it you need from us?" Champ asked.

"Figure out how we'll deal with this predicament. That Mexican cartel had a fraction of the wealth the Saudis have, gentlemen. We can't afford to lose their commerce. It will be tricky, but I have no doubts you'll brainstorm something brilliant."

"There's always a loophole, Winslow," Ira said. "Always."

"Make it clean and tidy."

"That'll be a challenge," Ira admitted. "Because we're fuckin' filthy."

Winslow turned to Ira. "Don't be crude. And don't be a fool. And for Christ's sake, most of all, don't be a hypocrite! Benevolence is not an attractive trait in our line of work. You know that."

He surveyed the water below. From this height, Miss Liberty was a toy that the grumpy old man could stomp on with the sole of his shoe, if he so pleased.

"By the way, Mister Mace," Winslow added, "I almost forgot to ask. How was the party you attended not long ago?"

Ira said nothing.

"Is it possible she and you are soul mates?" Winslow thought aloud.

Again, Ira said nothing.

"Champ," Winslow said, "do you know what the Latin word for gold is?"

"Can't say I do."

"*Aurum,*" Ira said quietly.

"Yes, *aurum,*" Winslow said. "Number seventy-nine on the periodic table.... We're landing, gentlemen. Take care of this rather large thorn in our sides and make M and J proud."

Twenty-Four

Nauseous and fatigued, Ira felt a slight draft pushing through his hospital gown at Sloan Kettering.

A chunky black nurse was typing his information into a computer. "Okay, Mister Mace," she said when she was done. "Doctor Greenberg will be with you shortly." She left the room, closing the door behind her.

Ira sat silently, depressed and alone.

Following a soft knock on the door, the doctor entered. "Good morning, Mister Mace. How's it going?" he said, before going over to the computer to read Ira's file.

For his answer, Ira pointed to his paper gown.

"Right."

Ira could tell the doctor wanted to say something, but was hesitating. "Go ahead. Say it, Doc."

"The prognosis is not in your favor, Ira. It's quite conceivable all of the partying and hard living you told me about have caught up with you. We found a rather sizeable malignant tumor in your stomach. That's why you've been vomiting blood. Not just the ulcers. I wish we had caught it earlier. According to your file, you haven't had a checkup in five years. Is that accurate?"

"How long have I got?"

"We have to see if the cancer has spread or not."

"And if it has?"

"You may have no more than six months. Even if it hasn't spread—if we go in and cut the tumor out, because of its sheer mass, I must warn you the surgery will be taxing on your digestive system. Look, I prefer to be up front with my patients. No matter how you slice this, Ira, brace yourself for a difficult journey ahead."

"I want the best. The best experts in the city. Money's no—"

"Good, Ira. That will unquestionably give you a better chance. But dare I say, money is not your primary issue."

"So, what's the primary issue?"

"Time. Time is the issue."

Ira loathed the facial expression Doctor Greenberg threw in his direction. Pity.

"However," the doctor added, "we're still waiting for more test results. And since money is not a concern, I'll look into experimental treatments your insurance might not cover. Don't quit on me. Bigger miracles happen every day, and there's still the possibility of getting out of this victorious. You need the correct mindset, though, Ira. You have to *want* to live. And any loved ones would serve greatly as positive reinforcement in this time of need. Why don't you get dressed and meet me in my office, okay?"

"Okay, Doc," Ira said despondently.

Twenty-Five

Ira savored a bite of his porterhouse at Peter Luger's Steak House. He set his fork and knife on the table and wiped his lips with a cloth napkin. Champ was sitting across from him, not yet touching his own steak.

"Nice and rare," Ira said. "Succulent."

"Is there a point to this meeting?" Champ asked with attitude.

"Yeah," Ira said. "I have news for you. And it ain't the good kind. Eat already." He picked up his knife and fork and went to town. Red juice from the steak ran down his chin.

"I don't think I can do this anymore," Champ said. "It's my last day."

Ira wiped his chin. "What are you talking about? It hasn't even been a year. Stop it."

"I'm dead serious," Champ said.

"Is it about what happened in the helicopter?"

"No…. Maybe…. I don't know."

Don't worry about that, kid. Just idle threats."

"It's not just about that."

"Good. Winslow and Britteridge can't intimidate us. I told those decrepit old mummies to go fuck themselves. I'm not giving them a fuckin' penny. Not one red cent!"

"Ira, I'm not sure that was a good—"

"More money? A raise? Huh? That's it, right? I agree, kid. You dealt with my bullshit, right? Double your salary."

"It's not about a raise, Ira. I'm telling ya, I can't do it. I'm not built for this."

"What are you sayin' to me? Eyes on the prize. Eyes on the prize. Keep pushing forward. Don't get caught up on things you can't control. You're on a mission."

"What's the prize for completing this mission, Ira? Tell me. What do you have? I mean, with substance?"

"Listen to this fuckin' guy," Ira said, as if talking to someone else at the table. He eyed his subordinate square in the grill. "You ever work a real day in your short measly life? Ever sleep on a bed of trash? Underground? In the fuckin' tunnels? I have. Shit! I conquered the globe, lost it, and got it all back! What have *you* ever fuckin' done, huh?"

"M and J doesn't give a shit about Americans," Champ said.

"Oh, a bank doesn't care? What a revelation you had. A bank doesn't care. No shit, Sherlock. Don't be a putz. It's not a person, Champ—with feelings. Emotions. It's utilitarian. Make money. Make money. Make mountains of fuckin' money."

"It's not right, Ira."

"Kid, pay attention. Let me enlighten you. You get one dance, Champ. You get one dance, and then you die a sorry death. *One dance*. And I'm gonna do the fuckin' Boogaloo till my feet are sore."

"You mean, fuck it all to hell."

Ira pulled out his ulcer medicine, popped some pills in his mouth, and tossed back his glass of whiskey. "What's with the dramatics? You're soft. What's wrong with ya, huh? You're twenty-one, for Christ's sake! You should be all piss and vinegar! What are ya? A pussy?"

"I'm not a pussy!" Champ shouted, causing the other patrons to swing their eyes in his direction. "I'm a human fuckin' being with a soul!"

Ira proceeded with his rare meat.

"Look at me!" Champ yelled, pounding his chest emphatically. "Right here! Right fuckin' here! You don't have the slightest clue about *that*, do you? Caring about others? An ounce of empathy?"

"What do *you* know?" Ira asked, pointing his steak knife in Champ's direction. "Got his hands a little dirty, and now he's ready to pussyfoot straight out the door. I love it." He laid his utensils on the table and raised his worn hands. "Any idea how much grime is on these? Do ya? Dirty garbage to dirty money! This life is dirty, no matter how you slice it! Accept it and move on!"

"What's wrong with you?" Champ asked, repulsed. "It's like you've been infected."

"Watch what you're sayin', kid."

"Infected with hopelessness.

"Pfff," is all Ira could get out.

"Painting everything as dark and opaque as onyx. But there's light. And there's love!" Champ calmed himself. "The most fucked up part is you're not as heartless as you pretend." Tears welled in his eyes. "I got a lot of love for you, Ira. You're like the only parent I have. But it really hurts. It hurts because I truly believe the world would be a better place if you'd never existed."

Twenty-Six

Wearing khakis, a polo shirt, and a frayed Yankees cap, Ira entered Grand Central Terminal. Normally so chaotic, the stunning station was moderately empty because it was past midnight.

In the subway a few flights below, he inconspicuously looked both ways, jumped onto the track, avoiding the third rail, and headed into the tunnel.

A warm breeze shot by as the ground rumbled underneath his feet. From around the bend, a 6 train's headlights flashed on his face. The conductor blew his horn frantically, but Ira didn't respond. He just closed his eyes. Stalling to the last possible second, he dodged the train by skipping over to the next track. Then he wandered deeper into the shadows.

"Ira? I don't believe it. Say it ain't so."

Tommy was sitting in the same old bunker with the same old dented lantern. This time around, his shades were different. He was now sporting circular John Lennon-type glasses with holograms of eyes on them.

Next to blind Tommy sat a man who oddly resembled Ira—that is, before he had cleaned himself up and became white-collared again. He assisted Tommy by lighting his pipe.

"How are ya, Tommy Boy?" Ira said, appearing from the gloom. "It's been a while."

"Boy, I assumed you kicked the bucket or somethin'," Tommy said. "You had me worryin'."

"Sorry," said Ira. "What happened was…."

"What?" Tommy asked.

"To be frank, I ran into a lot of bread. *A lot*."

"Good for you, Ira. You win the lottery?"

"Yeah, you could say that."

"I *did* say that, dum-dum."

The two yucked it up until Ira's shady look-alike awkwardly cackled, trying to join in the fun. Ira stared at the man with dismay.

"Where are my manners?" Tommy asked. "Oh, my goodness. Give the man that pipe to puff on."

"Nah." Ira let out a smile. "Not me."

"Oh!" Tommy yelled. "Here he goes! Rich man ain't smokin' no crack rock, is he? No, no, no, sir. But I bet you still be snortin' that good shit I told you 'bout. That flake."

"What can I say? You know me well, Tommy Boy."

Tommy laughed, followed by a cackle from his new buddy.

"What brings you to this part of town, huh?" Tommy asked. "The subterranean blues?"

"A couple reasons, I guess."

"Lay it on me."

"How do I put this?" Ira said. "Where do I start?"

"You're kin, Ira. You ain't win no lottery. You back to your winning ways, though, ain't ya? I remember you tellin' me about your life in finance. The big wheel turns by the grace of god. And the saga continues."

"I can faintly remember when I wasn't such a greedy green-eyed bastard. I wonder…."

"Wonder what?"

"What I would've been, I guess. What else I *could've* been."

"Makin' crazy coin ain't good enough?" Tommy asked seriously. "Here. I know you ain't too rich for some Jameson," he insisted.

Ira took a nip from the bottle. His chest slightly wheezed as he breathed out.

"That's what I'm talkin' 'bout," Tommy said.

Ira passed the bottle to his beat-up doppelganger, who still hadn't said a word.

"Must be great—all that gwap, huh?" Tommy asked.

"It makes you a servant of vanity. But it has its perks, too."

"Sexy perks, I bet," Tommy said. "Real sexy. Like Elizabeth Taylor. She had them titties, boy! Indeed, she did!"

"How would *you* know *that*?"

"Because I watched all her movies, dum-dum."

"You used to see?" Ira asked in amazement.

"Yeah, fool."

"I never knew," Ira said, astonished.

"You never asked. And when I could, I had a whole shit ton o' jobs. More jobs at one time than a Jamaican. But never a career. You got somethin' you're special at, don't ya? You rip 'em off real nice, don't ya? That's good."

"Is it?" Ira asked.

Tommy peered over his hologram glasses at Ira as if he could still see. "Shit, is it?"

"Shit, *is* it?" Ira's loaded look-a-like echoed.

"I see you found a replacement for me, huh?" Ira said, changing the subject after an uncomfortable pause.

"Him?" Tommy said. "You damn well know he's a few pineapples shy of a luau. It's still nice to have company."

"Yeah," Ira agreed.

"What's the first thing you wanted to rap about?" Tommy asked. "I don't got all night."

"I wanna get you outta here."

"Outta here? Where am I gonna go? You think of that?"

"I'll get you a place."

"Oh, you hear this shit?" Tommy asked his slow buddy. "He wants to buy us a place."

"Not *us*, Tommy Boy. *You*."

"I got no desires to leave here." Tommy tightened from frustration. "I don't know what gave you the idea I wanna. Besides, you don't know the rotten things I've done. I belong down here."

"Hades' Underworld," Ira said.

"Yeah. Whatever the fuck you said, smart guy." Tommy swigged from the bottle once more.

"Don't get bent outta shape. I had a hunch you wouldn't wanna go, but I had to try anyhow. For a friend."

"Now, what else did you wanna talk to me about, huh?"

Ira placed a padded envelope in Tommy's hand. "I need a favor."

"What's *this* about?"

"Keep it sealed," Ira instructed.

"What do I do with it?"

"I want you to mail this for me. But not now."

"When?"

"Six months. No sooner. All you have to do is drop it in a mailbox. *Any* mailbox. Ya think you can handle that?"

"Yeah, alright."

Then Ira handed Tommy a wad of crisp Benjamins coiled in a rubber band. The blind man unfolded the knot and counted each bill one at a time, making sure none were stuck together.

"Six grand," Ira said. "That's a G for every month you hold this envelope for me."

"Well, shit!"

"Don't spend it all in one place."

"You got it, cracker."

"I'm counting on you. Don't let me down." Ira hugged his old friend, speaking right into his fuzzy ear. "You're one of the few I can trust."

"No doubt. I'll help ya any way I can. I promise."

"Thanks for the good times, Tommy Boy."

"And the not so good times. Take care, Ira."

Twenty-Seven

In the dead of night, a Japanese beauty with tattooed sleeves strutted onto Ira's deck from inside. Wearing nothing but a purple G-string and a thin ankle bracelet, she joined Ira in the steamy Jacuzzi.

"What's your name again, doll?" Ira asked, drunk, puffing on a jay.

"Junko."

"I never seen you before down there... at Voodoo's."

"I'm new to the area."

"Glad you bought me a drink."

"My pleasure. You looked like you could use some company. Besides, I have an insatiable appetite for men with gorgeous eyes." She grabbed his dick. "And large packages."

"Junko, huh?"

"Yes."

"That's pretty."

"It means pure child," she said, taking a hit from the joint.

"Pure child? Well, your parents were way off wit dat one, honey," Ira slurred.

"You don't know the half," she said, before blowing the hit back into Ira's mouth.

Unable to control himself one second longer, he violently bent the alluring temptress over in the bubbling warm water, swiftly slid down her panties, and dropped his shorts. They fucked until she squealed in ecstasy, and Ira finished by squirting on her back.

"Why ya gotta scream out here, huh? I got neighbors, damn it!"

"Sorry, baby," Junko said, getting lipstick on Ira's cheek as she kissed him. "You fucked me so hard." Twirling her purple thong around her index finger, she walked back inside to rinse off.

After wrapping up with a towel, Ira stumbled into the apartment and sat at his desk.

"Alexa! The Clash!"

"Clash City Rockers" began to play throughout the loft as he opened a drawer, where his usual gang of scripts were, as well as a mirror with a pile of blow and a straw on it.

"Alexa, louder!" he yelled, wasted and woozy.

As Junko hummed merrily in the bathroom, Ira took out the mirror, whiffed a pinky-sized rail, and followed that with a handful of pills.

He stared at his computer for a bit, vigorously tapping his finger on the mouse, while hard-hitting guitar riffs strummed from the built-in wall speakers.

I quit, Ira read silently to himself from the screen. *I quit the easy way. No more games. No more fun. No more deceit.*

Still topless, the Japanese bombshell stepped out of the bathroom behind Ira and stealthily crept toward him, holding an icepick with a wooden handle by her side.

Almost sixty years, he typed. *Enough. Enough bullshit.*

Closer and closer Junko drew near, slowly raising the icepick and pointing it toward the base of Ira's neck.

This won't hurt at all.

In one fluid motion, Ira clutched a Beretta hidden in the top drawer, put it against his temple, and pulled the trigger. He slumped over his desk with half his skull blown clear off.

The erotic assassin wiped a small spatter of blood from her forehead and then took out a burner phone from her purse.

"*Moshi moshi,*" she said. "Yes. It wasn't as planned…, but it's done."

Twenty-Eight

Champ's plane landed at JFK. Waiting for his Samsonite suitcase at the baggage claim, he was startled by the pair of hands that unexpectedly covered his eyes from behind.

"Guess who?"

Champ's expression turned to delight as he realized it was Althea. They shared a warm embrace.

"How are ya?" Champ asked.

"Hanging in there," Althea said gently. "Yourself?"

"Better."

"Good."

"I needed a little space. To get away from—"

"Shhh. You don't have to explain," she assured him.

Champ lifted his luggage off the conveyer belt.

"Ready?" she asked.

"Yeah."

Before they could reach the sliding glass doors, a pair of undercover cops rushed up to them.

One of them revealed a badge from around his neck, waved it in front of Champ, and tucked it back under his sweatshirt. "I'm Martin," he announced. "And this is Mullins."

Mullins, also in plain clothes, nodded.

"What's this about?" Althea asked.

"You have your stuff, Champ?" Martin asked.

"There's a warrant for your arrest," Mullins said.

"On what charges?"

"Mitchell and Jones Savings formally filed charges against you regarding Mister Mace's affairs," Martin said.

Mullins added, "And since you fled—"

"He didn't flee!" Althea snapped.

"Since you couldn't be questioned, Champ, a warrant was issued."

"We would rather do this in private," Mullins said. "Let's not cause a scene."

Champ rolled his eyes at the lawmen. "This is crap."

"Let's get out of here," Althea said.

Martin clutched Champ's arm as the couple tried to head for the exit. "You're coming with us," he said.

"Man, get the hell off my arm!" Champ barked, breaking the cop's grip and slugging him in the mouth.

Mullins gave Champ a kidney punch, bringing him to his knees, then slipped in some more shots for his partner, prior to slapping on the cuffs.

"Don't touch him!" Althea screamed as Martin violently shoved her to the ground. "Get the hell off, you bastards!"

$

Champ soon found himself in a windowless airport holding room. He sat there quietly until a lumpy uniformed officer walked in.

"Alright, numbnuts," said the officer.

"My name is Champ."

"Champ of the dipshits!"

"Do me a favor," Champ said. "Don't stop your Jenny Craig diet. You still have a ways to go."

"Come with me, wiseass. Punched an airport undercover, did ya?"

Champ stood face-to-face with the officer. "Yeah, I did," he said.

"Well, you're a lucky man, asshole. You're free for now. Someone must love ya out there."

"Althea?"

"Who?" the officer asked, confused.

Twenty-Nine

Champ sat at a booth across from Catherine Finer.

"So?" Champ asked impatiently.

"So."

"This diner's a dump."

"We've been searching for you, Champ."

"Is that why you filed those horseshit charges?" He held his hand in the air. "Sally!"

A waitress with a nametag reading, "Sally," walked over.

"I want two eggs, sunny side up—extra runny," said Champ. "Add two orders of silver dollar pancakes, orange juice, and bring some of that burnt-smelling shit you call coffee."

"And you, miss?" Sally asked.

"Just coffee. Thank you."

The waitress finished scratching down the order and left.

"We had to find you as urgently as possible, Champ," Ms. Finer said. "You upped and vanished in the blink of an eye."

"I had to get away for a bit. After what happened."

"After your buddy blew his brains out?"

"Yeah, after that," Champ said, gritting his teeth.

"Apparently, he was quite sick already. If that makes you feel better."

The waitress came back with a pot of burnt coffee, poured them each a cup, and walked away.

"For what it's worth," Ms. Finer said, "I actually liked the prick. But he had a tendency to make bad decisions." She reached into her purse and placed a packet of papers in front of Champ. "Speaking of poor decisions, here's a copy of Mister Mace's last will and testament," she added, pointing to the packet. "You were one of only two beneficiaries."

"How much?" Champ asked, thumbing through the packet.

"Unfortunately for you, Champ, next to nothing."

"Nothing?"

"The private jets, the copters, the chauffeurs—you know he paid for none of those. His Tribeca loft was a rental. He owned zilch. I guess material things weren't his end goal. Like me, it's more about winning the game. About—"

"What did *you* win, huh?"

Ms. Finer's glare was intimidating. "About... being good at something. *Really* good. Purpose."

Champ shrugged dismissively.

"A shame," she said with a sigh.

"What's a shame?"

"It seems he donated the entirety of his legal earnings with M and J to a food shelter in East Harlem. Over five million left to an insignificant shanty, if you ask me. Pathetic."

"So, he left me nothing?" Champ asked. "I don't get it."

"I said *next* to nothing. He left you a safe deposit box at our midtown branch."

"He did?"

"Yes. And we took the liberty of opening it for you."

"What was in it?"

"A terse note."

"What it say?"

"It said, 'Fuck you, heathens!'"

Champ cracked a smile and slid the copy of the will across the table.

"Where's the rest of the money?" she demanded. "He stole it from us, and we want it back."

"How the fuck should *I* know?" Champ said defiantly. "He never told me nothin'."

"Time will tell if you're being truthful, young man. Time will certainly tell." She sipped from her mug. "I trust that when we part ways today, you will be able to keep your mouth shut about everything you've seen and heard."

"Here you go," the waitress said, setting a glass of juice and three plates in front of Champ.

Drenching his pancakes with syrup, he dove in.

"We've squashed stronger boys than you," the callous redhead said. "And I have no doubt we will do it again in the future."

"I'm shaking in my fuckin' boots, lady."

"Don't take me lightly, Champ."

"Who could take a shrewd she-devil like yourself lightly?"

"You know…, that girlfriend of yours is adorable. Sweet. Sweet but naïve. We've been watching."

That got his attention.

"Sweet and naïve," she continued. "Like you…. It's an ugly, cold world out there. The sooner you two realize that, the better off you'll both be."

"Thanks for the words of wisdom. And leave Althea the fuck outta this."

"Look, the bottom line is, we want to be done with Ira and his ties. This whole experiment, although lucrative, was a mistake. We're moving in a different direction and prefer his wrongdoings never bubble to the surface. Besides, Champ, most wouldn't want to hear it anyway. It's not pretty stuff. Right, sweetie?"

"Nope."

"We're dropping the charges against you. Keep your mouth shut, and you'll be fine."

Champ kept eating.

"Hey!" Ms. Finer said. "Tell me you'll keep your mouth shut. Say it. I want you to say it out loud."

"I'll keep my damn mouth shut!" Champ continued devouring his silver dollars. "And *you're* paying the fuckin' check."

Thirty

Excited that graduation was within reach, Champ finished his first day of the winter semester. Then he walked over to Tyler and Reese's messy East Village apartment, where he had been staying. His roommates were battling each other in a heated game of Madden Football, taking turns talking shit and trying to get under each other's skin.

"Hi, baby!" Althea said, heating a tea kettle in the kitchenette. "I just beat you here. There's a package on the table that came for you. Kinda weird—there wasn't a return address."

"And it looks all grimy and tattered up," Reese said.

"Like it came out a bum's ass," Tyler added.

Champ was puzzled. He tore open the padded envelope. Inside, wrapped in a dress sock, was Ira's gold Rolex. There was also a letter. It read:

Hey, kiddo.

I had to go. My days as a blood sucker have alas ended. Not sure if I'm heading through the pearly gates or down below to serve some time. All I know at this point is I won't be a problem to anyone anymore. With that said, it's time for new blood to come in. Impervious to the lore of crooked cheats like myself. Last time we spoke, you told me the world would be a better place if I had never existed. You're probably right. Now it's your turn. I leave it all to YOU. The People's Champ! So what's it gonna be, huh? Who will you save? What will you stand for? You tell me, kid. The next time we meet.

Love,
Ira

P.s. Aurum79. You know what to do...

Champ sat on the couch next to Althea, who was playing with his new wristwatch. After a moment, he lit a joint and slowly puffed on it, deep in thought. Then he grabbed his MacBook and loaded up a site he had used frequently—Cayman National Bank's homepage. Following a few failed attempts, under account name he typed in *ThePeoplesChamp*. Under password, he typed in *Aurum79*.

His jaw dropped as January's statement for The People's Champion, LLC popped up on the screen. The total amount available in the account read:

$$\$407,298,801.34$$

www.ingramcontent.com/pod-product-compliance
Lightning Source LLC
Chambersburg PA
CBHW071134200626
46817CB00018B/2948